The gloaming thickened.

And then a figure appeared.

A woman---old, thin, ghostly.

Veiled, she approached us from the north swaying, dancing without music, or no music that I could hear.

Seghers yelled at me: "Put your children in the tent! Get in there with them!"

"What is it?"

"Do it! Now!"

So I did.

I told our children not to be afraid.

But I was.

The woman continued to approach very slowly, weaving and bobbing, her face a mask of mist or smoke, no features clear and discernible except for small, burning red eyes. She wore a gray, tattered shroud---sinister clothing of terror. Then, as I continued looking out through the slit in the tent, I could make out more of her face, including a toothless smile from beyond the grave.

Seghers edged close to the tent.

"It is the Breath Charmer," he said. "A serious threat."

"What does she want?"

He did not answer. Instead, he called out something to the woman.

Momentarily she stopped, but then her dancing increased in pace and frenzy until an extraordinary development occurred: her hands caught on fire. I think that both Seghers and I were stunned as we looked on. When it appeared that her hands were black, charred gloves, her dancing ceased.

And I could smell her breath---fetid and poisonous: the perfume of misery.

I could see it. I could see it coiling out from her lips with a serpentine geometry, gray-white and thicker than rope.

Seghers leaned down and whispered, "She can strangle a person with her breath. She can spin a web around one and leave him to die."

Prolegomenon

The Empty Too Much is a fantasy realm I have always known but have never set foot in. My daimons of imaginative autonomy gifted it to me when I was a boy growing up in Kansas just down the road, in my mind at least, from Dorothy and Toto. The realm followed me to Alabama where now, as an older adult, I can no longer refuse the call to tell stories set in this mysterious and magical place. Visiting Africa several years ago galvanized my creative energies, and yet I waited for my brave unbodied scheme to pulse to life, for The Empty Too Much has taught me, above all else, that patience is everything.

While the narrative that follows should provide most of the details necessary for you to grasp the realm and the attendant rules of the fantasy, I would like to share the fact that my creation is very loosely modeled on the great Sahara region of northern Africa—just simply imagine that The Empty Too Much is larger, more incomprehensible and even more dangerous. It is a realm filled with as many stories as the night sky above us has stars.

The People of the Wild is but one of them.

It is a love story as well as an adventure story and a ghost story; it is a narrative of the courage required to face strangeness and the unknown while never losing faith in beauty and mystery. If this story should move you, remember with Emerson that it is because it has touched what is oldest in yourself. In essence, if it connects, it is because you heard it long ago and because it possesses truths you have always known.

—Stephen Gresham

1

Ⓜy Dearest Salmaya,

This morning, in a village without a name, I, your Mozef, discovered a tavern without a soul. A dark and smelly establishment, it lacked even the pretense of civility let alone hospitality. A wooden sign above a torch-lit bar eaten by shadows identified the watering hole as The Tavern of the Bones. Eerily displayed above the sign was the skeleton of a most unusual creature ten feet or more in length and four to five feet in height. It vaguely resembled a very large, prehistoric canine of some type—except for one arresting detail: the skull possessed an unmistakably human shape and countenance. The carefully assembled creature hung from an impossibly black ceiling by heavy ropes. Below the display was a question carved into a slab of polished, ebony wood:

"Is this a Man of Never?"

I thought it beyond strange.

You would understand what I had in mind as I pressed past a half dozen or more drunken men slouching at filthy tables, drinking varieties of alcohol the fumes of which gave off a poisonous stench. The men reeked even more than the alcohol.

A squat, roundish bartender rose from the shadows to meet my inquiry. The man evidenced all the animation of a dying animal no longer capable of resisting death; his eyes had lost touch with life; his flesh tattooed with rotting scabs.

"I need a healer," I said, and as I repeated the line, I tried and failed to rein in the anxiety in my voice. I did, of course, continue clutching the handle of my small, flat cart; its cargo stayed covered in a cloth, black hood. As I waited, I shifted the sizeable pack I was carrying, among its contents a satchel of your stunningly marvelous drawings.

The drunken men, their eyes the color of smoke, raised their chins just high enough to look at me with a mixture of indifference and pity. Had they heard strangers make such a request before? I wondered.

The bar tender obviously knew I was a first time visitor to The Empty Too Much. He surveyed my slender, unlikely frame and wiped his burly hands on a dirty towel.

"You should not have come," he said.

I leaned in closer and said, "But I was told that I could find a powerful healer in this realm. I need one."

The bartender's eyes were slow and watery.

"Go back. There's nothing for you in our land of nowhere."

And he turned away as if he assumed I would then vanish among the shadows. In the coalescing of those shadows with the light from low-burning torches on a far wall, a man materialized at a table; he was sitting between stacks of ancient-looking tomes and rolled up manuscripts. He was bearded, his eyes squinty from too many years of seeking something much desired among countless words; he seemed as distinctly out of place in the tavern as I. But feeling something like hope, I gazed in his direction.

The man, perhaps a desert scholar, for I'd been told The Empty Too Much attracts more than a few, had apparently been listening. In an intimate whisper, he said, "Death is the only healer in this eternal nothingness."

I took several steps towards him.

"That's not what they maintain where I'm from."

Another whisper in response: "The bartender is right. You should go back—to the other side of the mountain, I assume. You don't belong here. Many who arrive don't belong."

"What about The People of the Wild? I'm told that they are healers."

My reference caused the scholar to hesitate.

He seemed uncomfortable. He replaced his whispers with a clear voice: "No one absolutely knows whether they exist or, if they do, even whether they are wholly alive. They are written about in mythic terms. Legends. Desert folklore."

Then the man tapped the foxed and dog-eared cover of one of his books.

I tried to size him up.

Salmaya, I wanted so to believe he could help.

"I must find them," I said. "I have no choice. I can't go back."

The scholar studied me with the curiosity that he, no doubt, lavished upon his books and manuscripts.

"No one could harbor that much rashness, that much desperation," he said.

"If I could only hire a guide," I said. "I've been told that there are many skilled ones in this area."

By degrees, I could see the scholar being drawn to the black hood covering the cargo of my cart. Gesturing with an index finger, he said, "May I see?"

I nodded reluctantly. Should I have denied his request?

I watched as the scholar gently raised the cloth.

And I held my breath.

Although the man's eyes narrowed, he did not curse or shriek or scream. He did not shiver or grimace. He did, however, swallow with an audible click. Then—I can only describe it this way—his upper body suddenly was seized by a violent wrenching together of the shoulders. A convulsion. He released the cloth and reached for a drink from his canteen; but he seemed unable to grasp it as if his hands couldn't function, as if his fingers wouldn't obey. His was the image of one pulling his fears inside himself like a small animal backing into its hole for safety.

Ashen and sweaty, he closed his eyes and said, "No one here will help you." Then he lowered his head as if he desired never to see me and what was beneath the hood again.

Strangely enough, at that moment a large lizard skittered along the base of the wall to my right; as if in response to the creature, there was movement under the hood. A shuffling. Then one of those indistinct, yet bizarre noises I've told you about. Like an ominous grunt. Or a hiss of warning. A leprous wordlessness.

Still determined, I pulled my cart away from the scholar, parting the living shadows of men at tables where a nimbus of a yellow smoke hovered above them.

"I won't leave until someone offers to help," I said, raising my voice.

A young man, no more than a boy, with one eye gouged out, the wound suppurating, roused from his inebriation, reached boldly for my cart and clumsily lifted the hood. His scream was a knife stab of sound. Confusion exploded. Shouts and cries echoed. Some of the men drew the pistols of desert outlaws, some drew short but malicious swords.

With surprising quickness the bartender entered the tumult, yelling for me to leave; on a leash of unbreakable chain he brought with him a massive hyena muzzled with thick leather. Salmaya, there was a fire in the animal's eyes that could have melted stone.

The hyena lunged. I yanked at my cart and stumbled back.

There was more shouting. Anger was a chorus above the din of fear.

And then the inevitable: I was summarily driven from the tavern and told never to return.

In the piercing sunlight outside the establishment, I noticed gaunt women sweeping dust and sand from the entrances to their hovels. Pathetic children swarmed around me and my cart, their palms open, begging for a *bazarcht,* a gift; I had to swat them away. I hated doing so, but I had nothing to give. Salmaya, my heart went out to them; they were so hopeless as to be holy, like sacred innocents. Wary, whip-thin dogs barked at me, then fearfully shuffled a safe distance from my black-draped cart.

I didn't know where to turn.

Words and images of confusion spun dust devils in my thoughts.

"Is coming to this nowhere a mistake?" I asked myself.

I thought longingly of our home: The Land of Speaking Rivers.

So beautiful.

But then I glanced down at my cart.

"No," I said to myself, "there must be no turning back."
To you, my precious Salmaya, I make that promise.

2

Dearest Salmaya,

In The Empty Too Much, one hears impossible things.

As first light approaches, birds sing unfamiliar songs giving voice in that unpremeditated way you and I used to marvel at. But there's more: voices out of the invisible, for the sand here at my campsite stretches out like a table, visibility clear for miles. No one could keep from being seen. The source of these voices? I have no idea. I know only that they speak as if they are reciting verse. I wish you could hear them. Poets of the nearing dawn. A gathering of them. As such they call up memories of how much I always enjoyed hearing you read poetry. Hearing your soft tone as the words of fire consumed me as if I'd been dry grass.

Well, but never again to experience that.

I have pitched a tent less than a mile from the nameless village. The desert is surprisingly chilly at night. I believe I'm the only one of us awake.

So it's a good moment to share what happened yesterday after being chased from The Tavern of the Bones. As I've said, I was feeling helpless and hopeless. A stranger attempted to rescue me—a remarkably odd figure—a man who more than anything else resembled a giant lizard. His face, wrinkled and knobby and grayish, was elongated, his mouth sizeable and from which I half expected to see a slithery, forked tongue.

Emerging from a shadowy alley, he drew near and said a name: "Seghers. Piro Seghers." And when I naturally followed up with the obvious question, he said, He's the best guide you could possibly have.

"Where might I find him?"

"In the jail."

"Charged with what crime?"

There upon the odd man hesitated as if I had asked something quite difficult to answer. He slowly closed one of his large, dark eyes and said, "Madness, I would suppose."

I had turned away but a moment to look down the dusty, sun-blistered street in search of any sign of a jail. When I sought to ask more of this Seghers, the man had disappeared. I dashed into the alley from whence he had come only to catch sight of a scattering of lizards, possibly a dozen, gray in color and three feet or more in length. As I've said: no sign of the man.

With my cart in tow, I located the jail, a depressing hole of a place swarming with flies; the derelict building had three cramped cells, each with a floor of straw, each stinking of urine and who knows what else. The jailer, a bald man with pointed ears, led me to Seghers.

Salmaya, I tell you the truth when I say that the man appeared to be expecting me. He was sitting in a corner, his rough, dark hands cupped over his knees; his tattered robe was the color of mud. All in all it seemed that he was not simply a man who had lived many, many years in the desert but rather a man who was *inhabited* by the desert. The sun had burnished his face. Wind had carved his cheeks and forehead. White stubble flecked his chin and jaw and under his nose. But what marked my impression most deeply were his eyes: it seemed to me that they dreamed of eternity.

Even before the jailer could introduce me and inform him of my business, Seghers looked past me to my cart and in a voice grown old with words said, "Do you believe that Fate will sing us into the storm of her roaring world?"

There was more than a patina of lunacy in his preemptive comment.

I felt an instant aversion to him. Was it fear?

While I didn't respond to his question, I did explain that I needed a healer and that I needed a guide. A sane one.

His eyes, those dreaming eyes, smiled.

"Madness has never stopped the moon from rising," he

said, his tone the scratchy depth of a shallow grave.

I told the jailer that this was not the man I was seeking.

Seghers got to his feet and grasped the bars of his cell. With his stubbled chin he gestured to my cart.

"Have us a look?"

I allowed him to, hoping that he would be terrified.

Salmaya, my dear, the man did not wince or give any indication of repulsion or unease. He hunkered down and stared beneath the hood for a minute or more. Then he glanced up at me and sighed as if commiserating: "What do you have we here?" he said.

I thought of you, Salmaya.

I thought of all that had occurred five years ago. I thought of the recent sorrow that had brought me to The Empty Too Much. I saw that the desert madman truly wanted an answer. Perhaps had earned one.

"They are my children," I said, "and I would do utterly anything to save them."

"Then you should trust Seghers," he said, thumping his chest, "Seghers and the voices of the invisible."

"No," I said, "I'll find another way."

3

Salmaya, My Love,

I gaze at the beautiful face of dawn.

Wherever will the day take us? I hear our children rustling. Will they be hungry? I hope so. I cannot bear to see them wither further. The Wasting, that cruel affliction from which they have suffered for the past several months, siphons off their appetite. I must insist that they eat—a few dates perhaps or some spoons of watery porridge.

The Empty Too Much, in contrast, seems always hungry. I have learned right away that it is a place where one can be swallowed by despair. The ancient lifelessness surrounding us appears better suited for prehistoric creatures than for a man and his ailing children. But so be it.

Oh, Salmaya, when I remove their hood I'm greeted with the warm chortle of love, especially from Gela and Simeo. No, I must admit that Forg remains the quiet one, the distant one, ever the troubled one. I don't believe any of them slept well. I heard them cry out in pain once or twice during the night—especially Simeo.

Dear Father, Dear Father, says Gela as she taps gleefully at my beard. Simeo echoes her; he smiles as I move to where he can see me. Forg grunts discontentedly; his nose is running. I move around and crouch down in front of him to wipe it. His face is a mask of misery.

As I lift the children from the cart, Gela purrs like a kitten and Simeo chitters like a small monkey. Forg groans. I talk to them softly and kiss their fingers and the fine hairs on their mostly bald heads; I smile into their horribly wrinkled skin, taken aback as usual at the fact that while they are only five years of age, they appear to be twenty times that.

Salmaya, part of me understands why people abhor them. Why they are seen as a monstrosity. Nature's grave error. Child freaks. The single, central spine that connects the three of them seems normal enough, but the sight of two little boys and one girl, back to back, sentenced never to face one another makes most onlookers cringe. I'm thankful, of course, that each has two arms, hands, legs and feet, all mostly functional. But to punctuate the weird configuration of their deformity, Nature, as you've seen, gave them two additional legs and feet—one between Gela and Simeo, one between Simeo and Forg. The children refer to these extra appendages as *stummies*. I don't know where they found that term.

"Who's hungry?" I say.

Well, I do get them to drink some water. Gela and Simeo choke down one date each. Forg, however, goes back to sleep. As always, I must watch them carefully during the day. They're unable to take much sun, and the incessant wind and sand can also threaten them. I make certain that each is wrapped in a soft, protective robe of camel hair.

I try to start and end each day with the same words to them: "I love you three in one, my children of forever."

They are precious to me beyond words.

And this morning I tell them what I have concluded: "We need the man, Seghers. We need someone who can help us find you a healer." Then I fall silent. Gela and Simeo twitter like flightless birds. Forg continues to sleep; I can hear an ominous rasping in his chest.

So, through the heat and the wind, we return to the jail.

Seghers is not surprised to see us.

When I pull the jailer aside to explain that I have changed my mind about his prisoner, I expect him to demand money or something of value in exchange for the man's release. But there is only this: "Take him away," he says. "Place your hand upon my shoulder and promise that you will never return him."

I do as he prescribes.

To Seghers he says, "You and your madness are free to go

with this man. Know that when you leave this village, you leave an exile. Stay forever from this part of The Empty Too Much. Disobey, and you'll be hunted down, captured and hanged."

Seghers nods. He does not speak.

To me the jailer says, "May the forces of the divine protect you."

I feel alone with the Alone.

"Am I," I ask myself, "acting foolishly? Placing my children in danger?"

Oh, Salmaya, the oldest, deepest part of myself is unsure.

4

My Salmaya, Dear One,

We have entered an oppressive landscape of indescribable desolation.

At the start of this sacred quest to heal the children, Seghers said only this: "Let the wind of the unforeseen blow in our faces."

I did not ask him to explain.

It appears that we are following an old caravan trail south to southwest, I believe. For several hours I felt drunk on an untenable combination of hope and dread.

The void of the great desert holds us captive.

Seghers, however, displays no sign of alarm.

Thankfully, during a treacherously hot part of the afternoon, we gain the shelter of a trio of large rocks that materialized almost magically. I can only assume that Seghers knew their location and had been leading us in that direction. I give a spoon or two of water to the children; they lift their mouths to me like baby birds. While we sit and rest, I spy, off in the womb of a mirage, a band of wayfarers, oblivious to us, their slow steps taking them deeper into the unknown.

What is *their* story? I wonder. What is *their* quest?

The buzz of hordes of black flies sounds like meat frying in a skillet. But our children, Salmaya, are brave and resigned with a gleam of cheer in their eyes. Not so much Forg, of course; his breathing does, though, seem less congested. Gela is singing a ditty she has taught herself and Simeo—it's not in the language of Always; neither is it in the language of Old Sentences. Simeo sings along, then apparently forgets the words, thus sending him and Gela into a spasm of laughter. The two of them often seem to live in the bubble of a secret language. Forg chooses not to, I believe. I touch his shriveled hand. I give him more water. He burps. I rub his head. It feels as hot as freshly baked bread.

Salmaya, let me describe our curious group, for we have more living entities than just Seghers, the children and myself. Two animals—the property of Seghers—serve as our load bearers: one is a magnificent wild ass named Nightheart; his hide, butterscotch in color, is as smooth as silk, his mane and tail are as black as crows. What a strong, noble creature he is! The children adore him, and he them. We also have a single-humped camel known as Bloodfire, the name appropriate because the beast has the unusual coloration of dried blood. This camel, while sometimes a dependable pack animal, is not friendly; his voice is repulsive—I often think he is either crying out for help or being strangled or both. Mostly, I try to avoid him. I think he'd like to bite me. I warn the children to keep their distance.

Of Seghers, what can I say?

I know that I must trust him.

And I sense that his connection with The Empty Too Much borders upon the unknowable. Often I find myself believing that he engages in a mystical communion with sand and wind and sun and stars. He speaks the language of the elements. And there is this: my soul trembles when I ponder what the children and I would do if Piro Seghers should ever abandon us.

As evening approaches, and we light our fire for supper, I hug each of our children and tell them of my undying love for you, their mother, and I remind them that you are with them always. Gela sheds a quiet tear; Simeo mutters a few words that sound like a giving of thanks. Forg coughs and whimpers to himself.

And now night has suddenly fallen. The stars here are so close I can almost reach up and pluck them like fruit. The children are asleep. Bloodfire is chewing his cud. Nightheart and Seghers are roaming on the perimeter of our campsite, their purpose not to be shared. I stare into the flames of our low dancing fire. I breathe in the air of an imagined eternity and recognize that I shall never understand the tortuous, secret soul of this realm.

Never.

5

Dearest Salmaya, My Comfort,

When I ask Seghers about The People of the Wild, he is clearly annoyed. Only when I persist does he even respond: "They have power," he says. "Many powers, in fact. And much, much *strangeness.*"

"Are you afraid of them?"

He stops cinching up Bloodfire to face me. I believe I hear something like awe in his voice.

"They ask too much, he says. *Too much.*"

I drop the issue, for I'm learning that in certain spots of time Seghers elects to enter an almost deadly abode of silence. He closes the door behind him. At such moments I am not welcome.

Later, on our only water break of the day, I ask him to tell me more about the healer he claims he can locate. What I learn, Salmaya, is that our hope centers on one who is barely more than a child himself: the Gazelle Boy, he is called.

"He has the healing touch?" I say, wishing I did not sound doubtful.

"Believe it when you see for yourself," is the response of Seghers.

I gather that we are traveling to the home of a woman who apparently knows where the Gazelle Boy keeps himself. A necessarily secretive aura surrounds the boy—he is both feared and revered. There are those who wish to kill him because they believe he is possessed by demons. Others would hunt him down as a trophy or a bragging right, it seems.

We somehow survive another day.

Evening, Salmaya, is always the best time for conversation. Thus when the children have been tended to and Seghers has seen to the animals, he and I poke at the fire. Words come more easily as one shares the reverie of flames. Words sometime flow like the breeze that kicks up as midnight arrives.

I would like to pay Seghers for his services, but he will not hear of it. When I ask him whether his being exiled troubles him, he snorts and tells me that now as he nears his ninetieth year of life such things mean nothing. I did not realize that he had acquired so many years.

And when I allude to what I saw at The Tavern of the Bones—the skeletal remains of what might be a Man of Never—his face takes on the dark etching of weathered rocks: "Do not speak of them," he says. "Put them out of your mind."

But for some reason I can't.

I have more questions. Too many probably.

Fate, for one. Does he believe in it? I remind him of his first comment to me from his jail cell.

"Yes," he says, "but it comes from within us and moves out into our moments."

Salmaya, his wording strikes me almost as poetry.

"And the voices of the invisible?"

"You will discover them for yourself," he says.

We then sit silently and drink a final cup of tea. It is a companionable moment broken finally by something he says to me—something that catches me completely off guard: "At first light," he says, "I must speak to you of your children. A thing about them you must consider."

He turns away from my need to respond.

Why must he be so cryptic?

I despise that about him.

And I know that I shall not sleep well.

6

Dearest Salmaya,

Seghers cannot keep his fingers from touching sand.

First light found me waiting for him to wake. I watched impatiently as he stirred and then sat and shifted the nearest grains of fine sand from one hand to the other as if he were measuring the infinite.

Then, as if he had secretly consulted an oracle, he sought me out.

Oh, Salmaya, what he shared is too bitter to swallow.

It seems that in his many years of seeking out the far corners of The Empty Too Much Seghers has learned and has taught himself much about medical conditions. While he is not a doctor or a surgeon—and not himself a healer—he has the power to diagnose based upon experience and observation.

During our pilgrimage, he has examined our children closely.

And, in the briefest of summary, here is what he told me about them: that I will be forced to choose.

At first, I didn't fully grasp what he meant.

Or perhaps I did and rejected the dark implications.

Salmaya, it is the belief of Seghers that *only one* of our three children can be saved. He maintains that the rigorous healing procedure they must undergo—the spinal separation—makes it virtually impossible that more than one child will survive. When I press him as to how he can be so certain, he deflects my words.

"I have seen," he says. "I know."

When the children wake and I begin fixing them breakfast, Gela pats at my face: "Dear Father," she says, "you have tears." Simeo is likewise concerned; Forg listens and a weird humming is generated high in his chest.

I tell them that my tears come from joy—the joy from having such loving, beautiful children. Simeo chuckles as he mutters the word *beautiful*. He assumes that I am joking.

For the rest of the day, my steps through the dust and sand, wind and heat, are heavy and difficult. I try to think only of the promise of the Gazelle Boy. Surely if he is a great healer, he'll be able to save all three of our children. During a water stop at a small, abandoned oasis, I share my thoughts with Seghers.

"We live in mysteries," he says, "but wisdom has it that courage is superior to hope."

Gela. Simeo. Forg.

Oh, Salmaya, I could not possibly choose.

Could *you*, my dearest?

7

Dear Salmaya, Ever My Companion,

As I write this, I am sitting by an emerald green pool of water. What was once an oasis here is now deserted. Seghers assures me that the water is drinkable, partly because a clear stream bubbles up from beneath a layer of rock to feed the site. On the opposite side of the pool, Nightheart and Bloodfire are quenching their thirst; not far from them, in a more shallow area, the children are splashing and, by all appearances, enjoying themselves. Even Forg.

Seghers is watching them for me. I sense that he likes the children, or at least they interest him, maybe even astonish him, I believe. He claims that we should experience cooler weather today. He studies such things. Some days the sky of The Empty Too Much rises and shapes itself into a labyrinth of grandeur where a mystical blue thickens to conceal all the possibilities of the future. But in the eyes of Seghers, I see a man who respects the cloudless beyond of this realm.

Thankfully, there is only a light, pleasant southerly breeze. Early this morning we heard animals—the howling of wolves, the broken laughter of hyenas—and even the macabre hooting of a desert owl. Seghers killed a young crocodile, so we'll have some meat today. Oh, and around dawn, we saw a half dozen cheetahs tracking off not far from us. Beautiful, sinuous creatures, looking as if they had cosmetically applied that characteristic, black slash of tear dropping from each eye.

"Are they hunting?" I said to Seghers.

"Not for food."

"What then?"

"Seeking emotional contentment," he said.

I scoffed at that. But Seghers appeared to be quite serious.

"What does a big cat know of such things?" I countered.

After a calculated pause he said, "Have you ever eaten the heart of a cheetah?"

"No, of course not."

His face darkened grimly.

"One day you will. One day when you least expect it."

Seghers, I sense, enjoys toying with me. Baiting me. Most of the time, I listen to him with only half my ears. But I must depend upon him.

As we enjoy these hours near the magical pool, I cannot put choice out of my thoughts. What if Seghers is right? What if I were compelled to select one of our children to live and the other two to die?

I put that metaphorical sword over my head.

Here, my love, are some of my thoughts.

First, there is Gela. Her beautiful eyes open like roses. They are your eyes, Salmaya, dark and warm and connected to her heart. As a woman she would have your touch. As a woman she would offer passion to a man in gentle, eagerly meaningful ways. Would she not be the best possible choice?

But then I consider Simeo. He is spiritual, angelic. Every realm would benefit from his future adult presence. He is full of grace, a quality beyond words. He is kind, loving and giving. I could live, alive in a river of wind, with him as my choice.

What of Forg? A boy orphaned from joy. Angry. Sullen. He is so conflicted and self-loathing that in anxious moments I have to stop him from biting himself or from doing physical harm to one of the *stummies*. Salmaya, he needs so much love. And there is this: if I were to ask Gela and Simeo to choose, I am certain in my soul that they would petition for him—they would argue that Forg, freed from the triangle of their bondage, would be transformed into a different, stronger, more whole and complete boy—and then later a good man.

When my thoughts gather into a storm, I have to ask this: Would the most humane choice be not to save any one of them?

But no, fortunately that storm passes quickly, and I feel the relief of non-threatening skies and a more responsible vision of reality.

I need your wise consul, Salmaya.

Speak to me. Send your ghost to help me. Speak, my love.

Towards evening Seghers roasted the crocodile meat. It was sweet and tender. Each of the our children ate several small pieces. After our meal, they called for Grinner. That is their name for a flute-like pipe I play for them at times. As you know, I am not a musician, but the instrument emits dancing, lilting, pitchy notes that bring smiles to the faces of our children. They jounce around and clap their hands—sometimes even Forg joins in—and kick out with their *stummies*. And all is good. For a run of moments, they seem to forget that most of the world sees them as monsters.

In a much welcomed bliss, our children have fallen asleep rather quickly tonight. Nightheart and Bloodfire have, likewise, settled in. The hyenas and wolves hauntingly address a waning moon. They sound achingly lonely. I glance up from our sleep fire to see Seghers out where shadows press close to our camp. He is lifting his hands to the stars as if in worship. Do they have messages for him? I hear him begin to sing a song I have never heard. His voice scales higher. Is it a song of madness? Certainly it is one that does not sound sane.

I close my eyes and imagine the Gazelle Boy applying his healing magic to our children. I imagine them separate and whole. Am I wishing for what may be impossible? Yes, perhaps. The Gazelle Boy shines out from the center of my solar system of hope.

Then I think of you, Salmaya. I have with me the soft night shirt you used to wear to bed. It smells of you—the perfume of a woman who each day showed me in a thousand ways how much love she needed to share and that I was her choice.

8

Dearest Salmaya,

These are moments of inexpressible sweetness.

For much of the morning, I've been in my tent together with our children, for our travel is impossible until a sand storm passes. Seghers claims we are experiencing the phenomenon of *sand-driving*: a combination of dust and sand with dense, ground-hugging clouds of dust overridden by sand. The dust is virtually a choking mist. Very fine rock particles blend with that dust, and the wind shoves the mixture with tremendous force. Sand clouds hover above the lower storm. According to Seghers, when the upper winds drop in speed, an authentic sand storm will be birthed. If the velocity of the wind then suddenly strengthens, the sand particles will actually bounce, a situation much to be feared because the skin of the face and hands can be severely damaged by the abrasive particles.

But the children and I touch away our anxieties.

We are happily sheltered from the storm.

Using a salve that Seghers prepared, I am rubbing their blistered skins. They enjoy it; in fact, they coo like doves and giggle and chortle. Forg quivers. I believe that he suffers the most of all three of them in these harsh conditions. I must admit that the salve is rather stinky. It contains crushed vulture bone, honey and a bit of dung from both Nightheart and Bloodfire.

Even as I bond more deeply with our children, I think of you, Salmaya. While today offers unfriendly conditions, often The Empty Too Much can be breathtakingly lovely. I wish I could write you a coded love poem as beautiful as the dying of the light when we slow and choose an evening campsite.

And I regret not having a stronger organ of memory. What I mostly recall are broken glass pieces of the past. Nothing whole and complete. For example, I remember when you told me that you were with child—you mentioned that the coming birth arrived as a mysterious annunciation from some unknown source. Something that was a part of you and yet autonomous. And, of course, I remember witnessing your pain as you needed to be cut open in order for our children to enter this breathing world. I remember the awful morning that your midwife told me your death was emerging from within you.

I remember how calmly, bravely you spoke with me in your final hours—how we chose names for our children and how you pressed your sweet lips to my ear and whispered, "This is not their home. One day you will have to let go of them, for that is what love means."

I fought your words.

Oh, Salmaya, I continue to fight them.

9

Dear Salmaya,

We pass a vaulting of rock face where the full bodies of three maned lions—big males—have been carved. They seem to breathe. They seem to roar, distantly. I point them out to our children.

I ask Seghers, "Who created them?"

He pauses to study them as if for the first time.

"Visionaries," he mutters.

"Why did they do so?"

"Because they are slaves to mystery."

"Could this kind of thing be a warning to travelers?"

"Mystery," he said, "is *always* a warning. Or a promise."

We soon move beyond the carvings. We seek the one who can direct us to the Gazelle Boy and his healing ways.

To Seghers I say, "Can one ever feel that he belongs in The Empty Too Much?"

He turns, and his eyes reach far off into the distance beyond me. He shakes his head.

"No, we are passersby. And with that, we must be content."

My dearest Salmaya, we experienced something harrowing around twilight. A residue of terror clings to me even as I write this account. Late afternoon, Seghers suggested that we detour slightly from our path, for he wanted to avoid what he referred to as The Land of Fauns and Satyrs where there is much piping of madness. That land, according to Seghers, also borders an area where the sand has been pulverized to a white powder rather the consistency of flour—The Relentless

White Emptiness—and there the winds force the powder to rise menacingly like white steam.

But as the light began to fail, we were halted by a murderous-looking man in smelly rags toting a rifle. We had strayed on to the Camp of the Hunters. We would be asked to explain ourselves. And so we followed him—having no choice—to a small copse of thorn trees where a fire blazed; dark-browed strangers met us. They spoke with a morbid languidness in shifting tones of threat and belligerence. Seghers addressed them in a conciliatory voice, but I could tell that he did not fully understand their language. They seemed not bent upon robbing us; however, they did show an interest in Nightheart.

At one point, an older man, wretched and seemingly crazed, shook a rifle in our faces and pointed to a shadowy area where a large thorn tree stood. From what Seghers could gather, a young man accused of being a thief had been hanged. He was one of their fellow hunters. We could see the outline of his body, the neck being stretched so severely it resembled a bloody and desiccated coil of cable. From the knees down, he had no legs. We were told that they had been eaten by a pack of hyenas even as the young man continued to struggle to breathe.

It was a hideous sight. I apologize even for mentioning it.

Were we being held captive?

I was so frightened that I believed I would become physically ill. I stayed protectively close to our loved ones.

Then things turned deadly as one dusty scarecrow of a man sniffed at the black cloth covering our dear children; then his face wrenched into nightmarish facial grimaces and he spat out something incomprehensible in a barbaric-sounding idiom. He drew a blood-caked knife.

"*Pegonana dmu ezuri,*" he yelled.

Later I learned his words meant, 'things of demon beauty.'

Seghers jumped between him and our children.

Salmaya, I assumed the worst. I was petrified and ashamed of my cowardice.

But I found words. I pleaded with them. I told them of the mortal condition of our children and that I had come to The

Empty Too Much in search of a healer. I mentioned the Gazelle Boy as my only hope.

To my surprise, they listened.

And yet, I believe the only reason we escaped was that Seghers handed over Nightheart to them. That seemed to appease them.

Seghers then spoke animatedly to an evil-seeming man with a long beard, the gang's leader, I believe. Their exchange somehow resulted in our being let go. We were far from them before I found that I could take a full breath.

We made camp.

After I had seen to our children, I sat with Seghers.

"Do not speak so freely to men like that," he said. "Words are like ghosts—you never know when they might return to haunt you."

"But I spoke the truth about our children and about the Gazelle Boy." .

Seghers picked up a handful of sand and coaxed it to drop steadily through his fingers in hourglass fashion.

"Keep a grip on your courage," he said. "Do not let it slip away."

I nodded. Then I said, "I'm sorry about Nightheart. It must feel like a great loss."

His only response was this: "A fine beast lives in the open of its Fate. Nothing or no one can divide its sense of what it is."

10

Dear Salmaya, My Lovely Presence,

Seghers was right not to worry.

Today as the sun found the highest point of its path, Nightheart, a broken rope around his neck, caught up with us. Our children cheered to see him. Even Bloodfire seemed pleased.

Seghers kissed the nose of the magnificent creature.

Then he knelt down in front of him and gestured for me to notice something. I followed the direction of his point, and there I saw blood on both hooves.

I believed that his captors deserved whatever violence Nightheart had meted out to them.

Filthy beings. Have we seen the last of them?

11

Dear One of My Heart,

We are a family. Yes, a curious one.

Two men, three children and two animals.

What strange bonds are forged by living things!

Four more days have passed since Nightheart rejoined us. If anything, his affection for our children has grown. Often, on our rest and water stops and when we have set up camp for the night, he will let our children play beneath him; I see how careful he is not to step on them; he even allows them to tug at his beautiful tail. Seghers has kindly rigged up something of a saddle for them to ride upon Nightheart's back. They hoot and holler and enjoy themselves immensely—yes, to some extent, Forg, too—as Seghers leads the wild ass in a gentle circle out from the camp fire of evenings.

On Nightheart's strong back, they wave and call out to me: "Father, Father, do you see us? Do you see how far we are from the ground?"

As we slip more decidedly to the south and west, the heat is not quite so fantastic because a wind from distant mountains frequently cools the air. The sand dunes, however, are now larger than we have seen before. Naturally we skirt them, for some are hundreds of feet high and impassable for us.

Locked in the desert's secret alchemy, I have noticed that after a windy day the dunes will emit a low-pitched sound so arresting that we cannot hear each other speak. The eerie sound rises spontaneously and lasts for ten or twenty minutes. How to describe it? A moan. A groan. A puzzled sigh. Our children seem enchanted by it. Gela and Simeo have become quite skilled at imitating the sound, but Seghers surrenders to it, lapsing into a deep listening; it is almost as if, again, he expects to receive messages from the beyond, a realm in which our children and I would be trespassers.

Salmaya, you know that your presence is with us always, especially nights when gusts are too strong for us to sleep under the stars. On those nights, I snuggle with our children in our tent and we talk and hug. At times I wake and hear Gela and Simeo whispering in what I can only assume is their secret language. Perhaps they are praying or perhaps they are speaking to your ghost. I don't intrude.

Then first light can be a time when they wake and press at me with their tiny fingers and mouth an urgent request: "Mother Touch! Mother Touch!" I comply, for while some may find it ghoulish, I reason that our contact with a relic of you helps each of us in our grieving process. I keep the reliquary—a bark box— on a cord looped around my neck and concealed within my cloak. The lid of the box has carved upon it a guardian image that would, I believe, please you: it's of a spidery, trimanoid figure just like our children.

In the box is your ring finger.

I had it removed on the day of your burial. And now, after five years, it is a lovely white bone, smooth and delicate, and, for me and our children, it is profoundly sacred. I let each of them hold it and stroke it and be *touched* by it. Yes, we feel touched by it. Often Gela will kiss the relic and press it to her precious cheek; often her tears will fall upon it. Simeo appears to enter a trance-like state when he holds the relic in his open hand. I sometimes imagine that he undergoes a visionary experience and that when he exits from it his lips involuntarily murmur a recital of his inner journey. But as is usually the case, Forg elects not to touch the relic or even to acknowledge verbally that he has been touched by it. I have, though, seen him stare at it, and as he does so, issue a mournful kenning and shudder. He connects, I believe, but perhaps he is connecting only with his own darkness.

Salmaya, it is the close of still another day. Seghers assures us that we are within three days of our destination if storms do not delay us. He speaks in warm tones of the woman whose abode we seek—the woman who can help us locate the Gazelle Boy. The healer.

Gazelle Boy: he is the promised dawn for the health of our children.

Gazelle Boy: he is the light within the shadows of my doubts.

12

Dearest Salmaya,

"Where then shall we be brought?"

Each day this is my question. Asking it has become a ritual in concert with The Empty Too Much, a realm conducive to rituals that force one to expand his consciousness in order to fully grasp the beauty and lyrical strangeness and terror evidenced everywhere on our quest.

We have moved at a slow pace all this day because Seghers cannot resist wandering off alone from our path to read—or so he claims—the symbolic designs of sand ridges and ripples. I sense that something troubles him, but I caution myself against asking. If there is danger, he would, I believe, tell me.

Late afternoon we swung close to a massive dune where a half dozen or more frantic individuals were digging into the sand base. Three large men, several boys and one woman, each with a crude shovel, attacked the countless grains.

"What are they doing?" I said to Seghers. "The heat will kill them. Who are they?"

"Witch Diggers," he responded.

As we passed within a stone's throw of them, they barely noticed us, so intent were they to engage in their task. Seghers explained that certain groups of people in The Empty Too Much worship the greater dunes. Others, such as the Witch Diggers, believe the old accounts of desert witches having been buried in the measureless formations as punishment for their wicked ways.

"It is said," Seghers offered, "that the evil women were buried alive."

"Why are these people trying to dig them up?" I inquired.

"Because they have dark beliefs. Because they believe the bones of the witches possess supernatural powers. They are nothing more than grave robbers."

For several miles I continued to think about the Witch Diggers and about the role of bones in rituals and beliefs. At first, I thought of the group as most assuredly crazy, but then I stepped back inwardly and chided myself for comparing the sanity of one ritual against another.

Before the dying of the light, we encountered a breathtaking spectacle. Having breasted a rather steep rise, we looked down upon a waterless rill the course of which meandered through large clumps of desert grass. Then we heard thunder. Nightheart whinnied as if to alert us to the approach of something unusual. Seghers, with his wild talent for seeing much that cannot be seen, directed my attention to the far right. I saw a moving column of dust. A mirage? No, it was the approach of hooves. It seemed there were thousands of lovely creatures racing, indifferent if not oblivious, to our presence.

A flowing stream of gazelles.

It took a decided span of minutes for them to pass beneath us.

Oh, Salmaya, what beauty!

Naturally, I asked Seghers whether the massive herd might be connected in any way with the Gazelle Boy. He shook his head, but I could tell that the sight of those animals quietly thrilled him. And, likewise, our children smiled in wonder at the passing, thunderous parade.

After our supper, thoughts of The Land of Speaking Rivers stole over me. Of course, I thought of you, of our days together, and especially of the hour we met. Do you remember? I was helping my father—the Water Finder—and I had just celebrated my seventeenth year. You were among the water carriers working a new well, and even then your skills at drawing mysterious figures on the skin of wealthy women was winning acclaim. Your days as a water carrier were, as a result, coming to a close.

When I first saw you, I quickly turned away, for I had never seen such a beautiful face; and when I poured the fresh water from my goat hide cask into your decorated jug I was so nervous that I spilled some of it. Your smile seemed to retrieve every drop—that is what I imagined.

I knew immediately that you generated more than a fresh song my heart would sing. No, you were the song itself. The song in which I would sing forever.

Tonight, I thought, too, of your mother, Jamilia, and what extraordinary help she was to me and our children after your passing. She it was who convinced me to take our children over the Speaking Rivers Mountains, and into The Empty Too Much, where they might be healed. What I would have done without her support and encouragement I cannot say.

The children are asleep now. Desert days tire them.

I fear that they are being drained of energy.

They need the touch of a powerful healer.

I am having my final cup of tea for the day. Seghers sits across from me drinking from a bottle of blue liquid. Can you imagine this, Salmaya? He says that it is wine—*blue* wine! He refers to it as *the wine of immortality*. He asks if I would like a drink, but I decline to accept one. Yes, I am tempted.

For several nights now I have noticed that Seghers pours himself into a thick book, its pages tattered, and its spine broken. I long to ask him what kind of book it is, but I shall wait for him to volunteer the information. This particular night I witness something new: with a vulture quill and strong-smelling ink he writes in the book, pausing now and again as if he is composing. Is he, too, writing letters? To whom? Is there a ghostly love in his life? Has he lost someone? The Empty Too Much is the perfect setting for such a theme. His actions are a mystery—yet, what about Seghers is *not* a mystery?

Past midnight Gela and Simeo wake me. Forg is ill. I go to him and find that his eyes are swollen shut. I ask Seghers to help, and he does, bringing a small pouch filled with a whitish liquid of some kind which he dabs around both of Forg's eyes.

"What is the medicine?" I ask.

"It is from a night-milked goat," he says. "It contains many healing properties."

I find again that I must trust him.

This morning, dear Salmaya, Forg is better.

And so I question why I tremble within. No doubt it is because I experienced a dark, passing thought: 'what if one of our children dies?' The gods forbid—but what if it occurs? What happens to the other two?

So many unanswered and perhaps unanswerable questions.

13

Dearest One,

"When we love, we must transform ourselves."

Salmaya, do you remember saying that to me? Your voice had folds like silk. Often, when I was with you, I felt as if I were growing wings and could not resist flying into the skies of your love.

Yes, have a good laugh at my bad poetry!

Seghers claims that we are very close to our destination.

I hope so. The winds have picked up. Our children and I are weary of battling sand and dust and the threat of scorpions and vipers.

We need to be haunted by the ghost of a home.

14

Dearest, Dearest Salmaya,

We have arrived!

There is so very much to tell you, but at best I can only summarize and touch upon special moments that live so lovingly with me.

We are staying at a sprawling, sandstone and cedar timber abode on a rocky ridge above and slightly beyond a mostly deserted village known as Hennia. To the west, cedar woods spread up into a mountainous region of immense physical beauty. When we reached the abode of our destination, we were gifted with a most pleasant surprise: rain. Wet, cooling, much desired rain. I allowed our children a few moments out in it, for in all our days trekking into The Empty Too Much we had not experienced anything like the gentle shower that seemed to have fallen just for us.

And we were cheered and sustained through a delicious supper of meaty stew and fresh bread and some kind of red berries—very sweet—I had never before tasted. There was milk for our children and a strong, grainy ale for me and Seghers. Call it a feast, indeed. Oh, Salmaya, I felt such waves of relief and gratitude.

The woman of the house is Maeleeva, an aged woman, though a few years younger than Seghers, I believe. One's immediate impression of her is that she is witchy and very intelligent and quietly friendly. While she remains lovely, she must, in her earlier days, have been utterly stunning to look upon: the face and form of a goddess. She has gray hair that reaches her waist and blue-gray eyes that pull you in and make you feel accepted for who you are. And her hand is so soft and soothing that I found myself stammering responses to her questions of greeting.

Then a surprise much in excess of the rain.

Seghers lovingly tapped Maeleeva on the shoulder and said to me, "Mozef, this fine woman is my sister."

Sister!

We were standing there, with a good fire blazing in the hearth, flames of light bordered with shadows, and I could see it—the resemblance—in the following way: both Maeleeva and Seghers speak with their faces, often substituting a movement of facial muscles for words whenever possible. Also, a separation of words and gestures.

For both, every word is as solid as a stone and as insubstantial as mist.

Not long after our arrival, we were joined by a man—a map maker—who was introduced by Maeleeva as her companion. His name is Treml. His long, reddish hair and beard and his pale skin shout out that he is from some northern realm, a cold realm, no doubt, and far, far from The Empty Too Much. He is somewhat short and troll-like, but from his handshake I sensed physical strength. Beyond that—is he unfriendly or merely shy? I can't be certain. I noticed that he and Seghers did not shake hands or exchange words of greeting. They merely nodded, their eyes brushing before looking away.

Maeleeva and our children bonded instantly. She seemed, indeed, to be able to speak their secret language. Certainly she gave no indication that she saw them as ghastly or even as anything but small children desiring to be healthy and to be loved. Gela and Simeo were especially pleased to meet Maeleeva's pet, a large, orange, long-haired cat with one eye (lost to a viper bite!). The cat's name is Drift, and I sense that Forg is a bit afraid of it.

Night came upon us quickly.

The children being tired, we fashioned a sleeping pallet for them, and they soon were sound asleep. Treml had, I assumed, returned to his map making room; Seghers had gone out to feed and water Nightheart and Bloodfire. Maeleeva did not have to coax me to sit up with her by the fire and talk.

"You know why Seghers has brought us to you?" I said.

"Yes. You need a healer."

"You see the condition of my children?"

She nodded.

"They are, sir, very sick. Very sick. The Wasting. They haven't many days."

Oh, Salmaya, her words burned at me as surely as if I had placed my hand in the flickering blaze.

"How many? How much longer?"

She did not hesitate.

"No more than two more moons. As few as fifty days."

I felt that some unknown force was strangling me. She reached out and touched my wrist in a gesture that felt as if she were rubbing a magic balm onto my skin. She assuaged many of my raging fears.

But I still had to clear my throat of rising tears.

I asked her about the Gazelle Boy, and I gasped when she said that she didn't know where he was at that moment. She did, however, explain that she frequently possessed the vision of a seer. That, if circumstances permitted, she could reach out with her mind to locate him.

I felt much better.

Then I asked her about The People of the Wild.

"Do you know them?" I said.

"No. But no one truly does."

I told her of the doubts Seghers harbored about them. Looking me squarely in the eyes she said, "If the Gazelle Boy fails, seek them out despite what Seghers might say. Have courage."

I mentioned that Seghers embraced courage.

Again she nodded. She glanced over at our sleeping children and said, "Talk about your departed wife, please."

And so I did, short of things most intimate. I spoke of your having been an orphan and of how your mother, Jamilia, was truly like a birth mother for you. I spoke of your experience of something like an annunciation regarding the coming of our children.

"You know nothing more?" she said.

I could not understand what she meant, and so I changed the subject to Seghers. She reaffirmed all my readings of him as mysterious.

Then I said, "He does not seem mad. Sanity lives in his days—I see many of its traces."

Maeleeva smiled wistfully. "They say he's mad because he listens to the gods of the invisible."

"Lately," I said, "I have seen him write in a thick, very old book."

She clapped her hands softly. Her eyes danced. "I'm glad to hear that he continues to take dictation."

"Dictation? From whom? What source?"

"Those same gods."

"What precisely is he writing down?"

Her gaze into the flames suggested a moment of holiness she could only share with the self she was before her birth. Then she caressed the firelight with her voice.

"Poetry," she murmured.

And her smile was gorgeous.

15

Dearest Salmaya,

After breakfast, Maeleeva excused herself to make her way up through the cedar forest.

"Where is she going?" I said to Seghers.

"To visit *Otherness*." Then, when he saw that I obviously did not know what he meant, he said, "She's gone to her secret spot, an isolated area where looking is not enough—where she must see with her heart."

"To locate the Gazelle Boy?"

"Yes." Over a cup of tea, he searched my face before adding, "Think your best thoughts for her. Your quest depends much upon her success."

"I will."

He suddenly seemed nervous, even a bit distraught.

"And do not," he said, "ask her questions when she returns."

"I will not," I said, though I nearly choked on those words.

I had to know. I had to.

As the day passed, Seghers and I restocked our supplies of food and water and anything else he deemed necessary to continue our journey. Treml kept to his work room where, I gathered, he spent much of his time preparing skins upon which he would draw up his maps. I wondered, of course, whether he would be drawing one for us—one that would show us the way to the Gazelle Boy.

For a good number of hours the children enjoyed playing with Drift.

I watched them and tried not to think about Maeleeva's

projection of their waning days. Salmaya, Salmaya, I must do everything possible to get these remarkable children well again.

I cannot, I must not, allow them to die.

I will always, always, always love them.

As I know you always will, too.

When we had enjoyed another delicious supper, I saw Seghers remove himself to a corner away from the hearth, yet still close enough to receive light. He thumbed through his old book; his lips moved as if he were reading intensely. His brow furrowed.

Poetry?

That was Maeleeva's claim.

The gods dictating to a mad man? It seemed improbable.

Before our children bedded down for the night, Treml brought out a stringed box and strummed it, and I tooted on Grinner. Gela and Simeo sang little ditties and filled their faces with smiles. Forg looked on as if he dearly wished he could share their joy.

Later, as Seghers, Treml and I drank too much ale, Maeleeva treated us to song—Salmaya, I tell you true, she has a hauntingly lovely voice. Of what did she sing?

Of the stars and night and desert winds and the sanctity of the heart.

And of much more.

But I did not ask her if she had received a vision of the Gazelle Boy's location. Oh, but how I wanted to! I did, though, whisper something to her before turning in: "Are we definitely on our way to the place of healing?"

She smiled a smile that touched my soul.

And whispered in response: "The god is the place that heals."

16

To the One Who is Always Near,

Salmaya, last night I dreamed strange dreams—one of the Man of Never or of a creature very like what I saw above the bar at The Tavern of the Bones. I was in a cave, and the creature approached, and I thought that I would be killed and eaten, but instead, it turned, having stared at me as if, indeed, it pitied me. I awoke, shivering, then I fell asleep again and dreamed that a lone cheetah spoke to me in a voice that I felt was reassuring, though I can recall nothing that the big, beautiful cat said. Such weirdness! Do dreams truly portend anything?

I do not know. But I recall that you believed in them.

This morning I awoke early and helped Maeleeva bring in water for the breakfast cauldron. She has a remarkable ability to get a blaze started in the hearth. I mentioned my dreams to her, and she simply smiled benignly, and then for some reason I mentioned Seghers: my appreciation for his helping me and our children. But, again, I voiced a certain regret that I did not understand him.

"He has secrets," she said.

"Any that I should be aware of?"

She looked away.

"In time, you will learn of several. Don't be alarmed by them."

Salmaya, you see that she is every bit as cryptic as her brother, and yet she wears it much more warmly than Seghers, and so I don't mind.

After breakfast, she told me that she wanted to spend a good part of the day with our children and that she wished for me to speak to Treml who had prepared a map for us. That, of course, gladdened me.

The Gazelle Boy—it suddenly seemed truly possible to find him.

That afternoon, I sought out Treml in his work room, a poorly lighted area that smelled of animal skins and pungent inks. I was surprised to discover Seghers there leaning over a map with Treml—they were speaking in hushed tones, both pointing at certain areas on the freshly unfolded document. When Seghers saw me, he rolled up the map, thanked Treml rather curtly and brushed past where I was standing.

"Now we will seek out your healer with confidence," he said.

Treml stood with his back to me in front of a map that covered every inch of the wall; it appeared to be a map of The Empty Too Much in its entirety. Salmaya, it was most impressive, such an expansive area—it made one feel small. When Treml turned to face me, he gave off the impression that I somehow confused him. I could feel it.

"So you're from The Land of Speaking Rivers—why ever would you leave all that green for our desolation?" he said, his shadow looming and ominous.

"For my children, of course."

He worked his fingers together rather impatiently. I had no idea what he was thinking. Then he stepped closer to me and said, "They must heal themselves."

"But how?"

He only nodded and said again, "They must heal themselves."

Salmaya, I tell you, I did not like the man. But somehow we were able to shift into a discussion of maps, and I began to study the large one and, in particular, gave my full attention to a designation in the far west—The Black Mountains—and, beyond the mountains, one identified as The Land Where the Dead Wind Speaks. I couldn't resist asking him where on that map one might locate The People of the Wild.

"There," he said, pointing at those mystical-seeming mountains.

He would not volunteer anything more specific about

The People of the Wild; instead, he surprised me by sharing a quest he once longed to make but that now, believing he wasn't physically able to, he wanted to hire a troop of younger men to carry out for him.

"Into The Land Where the Dead Wind Speaks," he said, "a terrible realm."

"What's there?"

He squinted at me. Then smiled, shook his head. A hint of fear crawled into his voice.

"Men of Never," he said. "That is what I believe, but almost no one else has that belief."

"Do you want to capture one?"

He did not respond.

Then, clearly, he was through talking. Abruptly, he broke off our time together and ushered me from the room. Any further questions I had buzzed about in the ensuing silence like insects.

What a curious fellow!

Our final evening with Maeleeva and Treml caught me up in an odd gloom.

I knew I would miss them.

Around the after supper fire, Treml told a bizarre northern tale about men who chose to become birds and yet found themselves longing for earth. I did not fully understand the meaning of the tale; I did not, however, ask for an explanation. And I was additionally puzzled when Seghers, being perhaps a bit too much in his cups of ale, said, "He who is not a bird shall not dwell over abysses."

I laughed softly, embarrassed for him, I suppose.

Then Maeleeva drew me aside to where our children had bedded down, though were not asleep. She showed me three round rocks rather like small, almost colorless marbles. Then placed one of the rocks in the mouth of each of them—obviously she had taught them how to hold the rocks so that they would not swallow them.

"This will help them," she said, "to learn to be silent. Silence is their much needed companion until you meet up with the Gazelle Boy."

Not for a second did I fail to trust her.

17

Dearest Salmaya,

Mysteries upon mysteries!

Before the sun was serious in its rise, we were off.

But I must put in this letter one most curious scene I observed at first light. I was headed out into the rocks to relieve myself when, off below a ways, almost hidden by a trio of cedars, I saw Maeleeva and Seghers.

I nearly called out to them a morning greeting.

I'm glad now that I did not.

For I saw them warmly embrace. And it moved me to see such a strong, brother-sister relationship.

And then.

And then—truly I do not lie and I do not believe that my eyes deceived me—the embrace flowed into a passionate kiss. A long, passionate kiss. The kiss, unmistakably, of lovers.

Not of brother and sister.

Ashamed, though rooted to my spot, I watched them kiss several more times with an ardent desire for one another, until finally Maeleeva pulled away, then reached up and caressed the cheek of Seghers in a gesture of unreadable closure.

He lowered his head as if immeasurably bereft.

18

Salmaya,

More and more the beauty of this journey emerges from the unpredictable intimacy and estrangement of what I see.

We are back in the desert.

We are apparently headed for a mountainous territory on the far horizon.

This morning I was awakened by the sound of what I can only characterize as mad sorrow: Seghers on his knees off away from our campsite, wailing and slapping at his body.

I knew that I dared not go to him.

I decided, as you must assume, that I would not admit that I had witnessed the scene between him and his sister.

Later, when I was feeding our children their breakfast, Seghers, as if almost alive, stumbled back to our small fire. He looked at me, and in a toneless voice said, "It is a wise saying: Without the pain of love, the heart is hollow."

19

Dearest Sweet Salmaya,

    I sit at the first fire of the day; the air is cool, and our children are still asleep. Seghers, roused from his bed earlier, has now dashed off towards the foothills trying to retrieve Bloodfire. It seems our unruly camel took it upon himself to escape from camp. Seghers believes he smelled a female not far away.

    There's something deeply contrary about Bloodfire; he's almost always in a bad mood these days. Much too frequently, Seghers is driven to whipping the poor beast just to get him to complete his daily tasks. I hate to see the beatings, but I suppose that they are necessary. At times, Seghers threatens death. Nightheart, on the other hand, is totally opposite in mood and behavior. As you might gather, our children and I have grown quite fond of him; a few moments ago, in fact, I went to Nightheart, and he let me rub my cheek against his. In his strength and grace, I feel a curious reassurance. While standing there next to him, I thought I heard a strange bird singing happiness older than the rocks or the sky or any body of water.

    In our quest to locate the Gazelle Boy, we are gaining elevation. There is less sand and more scree and fragments of ancient lava flow from extinct volcanoes, some of which loom on the distant horizon. We have seen herds of zebra and gazelles and even a foursome of desert elephants—seeing the latter was a delight for our children.

    As I sip my hot tea creamed with goat's milk, I think of you, dear Salmaya, and mutter promises that our children will soon come under the healing touch of the Gazelle Boy. Each day I grow more eager to see our children free from their life-draining affliction. Though I try, I cannot keep from thinking about Maeleeva's pronouncement regarding the limited time our children have if they are not treated.

I confess, as well, that I continue to think about her, and especially about the passionate moments between her and Seghers that I witnessed. What does it all mean? And could it be that what I saw is truly at the heart of the madness that our guide harbors? If so, I feel a profound sorrow for him. I'm quite certain that in The Empty Too Much a sexual love between brother and sister would be forbidden. I also wonder about Maeleeva and Treml—they do not seem a couple in virtually any respect. Why are they together?

Secrets. Too many secrets. Too many unknowns.

Other thoughts wing through my mind: The People of the Wild, The Black Mountains, the Men of Never and The Land Where the Dead Wind Speaks. Such mysteries. They excite me, and yet they sometimes cause me to shiver.

Well, my dearest, I hear our children rustling awake. Gela and Simeo are singing their morning hymn. When I once asked them the message of their hymn, Simeo explained that it was their wish that our tiny caravan encountered goodness during the hours to come. They sang out for the presence of goodness.

I must learn their hymn, for I, too, long for goodness to arrive.

Leading an uncooperative Bloodfire, Seghers is heading this way. He is swearing in both the language of Always and the language of Old Sentences. I must see if I can, if possible, help; at least I can pour him a fresh cup of tea.

More on our children: they continue to follow Maeleeva's prescription on keeping a rounded stone in their mouths for much of the day. The additional silence seems to have a positive effect on their physical as well as mental condition. Forg, of course, has some difficulties with his stone; I see him, every so often, take his from his mouth and hold it in his hand and stare at it as if it's a dead insect.

I also notice these things: from listening and from being still, our children make new words that only they can hear, words that rise from the three of them like steam or mist, words that make no sound but that generate echoes. And some days our children cast no shadows—what does that portend? I believe it frightens Seghers.

Our children: Is their childhood a mirage?

Some days I feel that they are already ancient.

20

Dearest Salmaya,

Two more days have passed.

Seghers says to me, "You're thinking that it's too far for you?"

Dawn pours fiery light and a promise of heat gathering between needles of rock from long ago volcanic eruptions. Rock: fractured, weathered, tortured; rock, mother to strange formations, geological children one could abide but not love.

Washing yesterday's dust and grit from the eyes of Gela, Simeo and Forg, I watch Seghers expertly load up Bloodfire, and I think about his question.

And I say to him, "Too far? What do you mean?"

Seghers swings his gaze away from the rising sun and towards a scattering of shadows doomed to disappear soon.

"Out there," he says.

"For the good of my children? No."

"I don't mean *them*. I mean *you*."

In the face of my sudden, deflective hesitation, Seghers barks at Bloodfire to get to his feet. The man has pieces of desert philosophy he feels compelled to share.

"Sometimes," he says, "a man gets lucky. He journeys into a honey-like darkness. Sweet on the tongue, you see."

And so I decide to play along.

"That kind of darkness—is it on any map?"

Seghers smiles through white stubble.

"Yes, on a map of incomprehensible strangeness, but no one has ever drawn that one or Piro Seghers would know."

"Not even Treml?" I say. When Seghers glares back at me, I add, "Are you telling me that we are at the mercy of luck?"

A rare chuckle in response.

"Oh, by the cursed blood in our veins," he mutters, "we are at the mercy of *everything*."

21

Salmaya, My Dearest,

Three more days have passed.

Sunset burns the last dust motes of the day, and I sense that I have been approaching this dying light since before I was born. Fate? Destiny? Our children hold tomorrow in their little, pathetic, beautiful hands. Or is it the other way around?

Night found day uneventfully.

But this is not a good morning: the eyes of our children reflect something gone or missing. Seghers frowns at what he sees. Even Nightheart is aware of what is not there—I wish that he could name it.

And the desert wind storms without end, without end.

After breakfast, Seghers hunkered down with his back to that wind and studied our map. He looked around as if seeking landmarks; the stony cast of his lips raised a bit of alarm in me.

"Are we getting closer to the Gazelle Boy?" I said.

His eyes pressed out a weak smile. He lifted a hand and pointed west.

I feigned confidence.

I glanced down at the map, and curious words rose in my thoughts: *Perhaps life is unmappable.*

The vultures of morning ask vespers of death. In a many-angled round, they wing high in a brightness brighter than my eyes can grip. Then they fall in a new geometry, calling out beneath them: there, there, over and over. Landing, they applaud the dead.

For a number of hours we angle more north than west.

We leave rocky scree and judder over small ripples of sand. As always, Seghers stops to read these formations as if he is explicating them. In the distance there are magnificent sandstone outcroppings. Could they be the abode of the Gazelle Boy?

Dear Salmaya, I pray that they are.

Towards the end of day, the blue above us darkens, invites stars, and the west leans over our miseries, our joys. I seem to hover just above my life, searching for a place to touch down. Then we sup. Seghers tends to the animals and I to our children. We worship the promise of the Gazelle Boy. The desert assails us with peace, and the left hand of approaching night is a silver glory.

For several hours beyond sunset now I've heard a mournful warbling spilling out of the rocks towering ahead of us.

I say to Seghers, "What is that? A bird of some kind?"

He listens. His ears catalog the sound.

"It is the bird of the red hour."

I assume that *red hour* means sunset.

"Why that song? It's so plaintive."

I sense that Seghers has heard the song many times before.

"It sings of things that have forgotten the way," he says.

"Why must it be so insistent in its song?"

Seghers closes his eyes as if he is searching for a completely different kind of answer. At last he finds one: "Might it be that your bird is crying at the edge of night for a dawn of hidden jewels never to be discovered?"

I don't pursue his imagery. He is, I believe, troubled about something.

In our tent Gela says, "Dear Father, are there rainbows on the moon?" Simeo reaches around for her hand to caress and kiss. Forg grunts dusty moments of disgust, or, at least, what sounds like disgust.

I smile into Gela's face. "Yes, there are," I say. "And every beam of moonlight has your name written on it." I tap her nose playfully.

"And the names of my brothers, too?" she pleads.

"Yes."

She hugs my neck and blinks away her tears, but Simeo—always a softy—sobs gently; Forg issues a gagging noise to protest my sentimentality and the emotional response of his siblings.

Suddenly I'm at home in my deepest affection.

"I love you, three in one, my children of forever," I say. "And I always, always, always will." Then I repeat my words, this time shouting them because I am bursting with feeling.

Seghers pokes his head into our tent, looks into my eyes and nods his approval, I think. And somewhere out in the night a lone hyena laughs darkly, longingly at the echo of my declaration.

Our children sleep.

But I can't, and so I fix another cup of tea for myself and Seghers. He is pacing about, smoking his desert weed cigarettes. I believe he is worried about our water supply which is quite low. Then he stops, looks in every direction, swears; visibly upset, he sits by the fire and stares into the flames.

He does not glance at me.

He tosses his cigarette away and shrugs.

He continues to keep his eyes on the gambol of the small fire.

In a strained whisper laced with the onset of fear, he speaks. "We are lost."

22

Salmaya, Dearest Love,

It is mid-morning, very warm, but, thankfully, little wind.

We are approaching what resembles a sandstone castle, the rock turreted and cut in arabesques and grotesques. Does a benevolent king or queen await us? Or will we be consigned to a dungeon of despair?

Our children, concealed under their black hood, ride on their cart, silent except for some barely audible exchanges between Gela and Simeo. I have not, of course, told them that we have lost our way.

Even the words themselves are the color of despair.

Seghers leads Bloodfire while I lead Nightheart who, in turn, pulls the cart. At first, I was angry with Seghers; I blamed him for our situation. A few minutes ago, I apologized. I am thirsty for hope.

Most of an hour later Seghers halts. It seems an odd place for us to stop. I see that he has raised one hand to shield his eyes. He is looking, looking, looking at something at the base of the sandstone formation.

I trust it is not a stony dragon guarding the castle.

I call out to him: "What is it? What do you see?"

And, to my great surprise, he starts to jig. Imagine that. Seghers dancing and cheering and laughing and applauding. I drop Nightheart's rope rein and catch up with our guide.

He continues to celebrate something.

"What?" I say. "Has the desert stolen your senses?"

"Fortune, fortune, fortune," Seghers cackles as he claps and hops from one sandal to the other as if the sand is burning his feet.

I grab his arm.

"What is it? Damn your spirit, tell me!"

His face awash in a smile, he turns and places his hands on my shoulders.

"It is *Waralibi.*" He shakes me as if to jog my memory, but the word he spoke means nothing to me. Then, his face close to mine, he says, "This is our good fortune, a stroke of good luck. *Waralibi.*"

"What is that word? What are you saying?"

"*Waralibi.* A man, but not an ordinary man."

And then I can see a tiny, dark figure standing by an arrowhead-shaped rock.

"You know this man, then? Who is he?"

Seghers lifts his hands from my shoulders, thrusts them at the sky and exclaims, "No ordinary man—he is *Waralibi.* He is The Listener at the Stone."

23

Dearest Salmaya,

The monolith was black like obsidian and, as I said, shaped like an arrowhead. It appeared that it had been fluted and grooved and cut upon with steel spikes. To touch it, to run one's fingers over its strange surface was, I swear to you, like making contact with something unworldly.

It was Waralibi's stone.

It stood alone rising ten to twelve feet, I believe. It was like a totem. It seemed magical. It *is* magical, according to Waralibi. It loomed above our fire, a sentry against the night.

But all is well, my dear, for it is now evening and our children are settling towards sleep. There is a cave here at the base of the sandstone; it is Waralibi's living area. I have pitched our tent within its walls. We have eaten well and had more than plenty of water. The cave protects us from the evening wind.

After calming down our children and saying goodnight to them, I go to sit at the fire with Seghers and Waralibi—The Listener at the Stone. Oh, Salmaya, what a bizarre figure is our savior, a man who now is squatting down, nursing the flames, gazing in at them, not lost in thought, it seems, nor oblivious, but free and untroubled as if he were alone with nobody around to observe him—the world of The Empty Too Much offers itself to him unmasked.

How to describe him? Well, he is rather short and very dark complexioned and manifests something of a hunched back. Despite the desert warmth, he wears a gray fur coat. It smells of dead animals and is animated by a riot of countless fleas. He has arms stunted in length and quite small hands and small, bare feet. His face is anchored by a prominent, pointed nose and a slit of a mouth that fails to hide large teeth. I should add that there are wild, unruly hairs growing out from his nose, a half dozen or so. His eyes are black and beady. His ears—well, his ears are the all and all of his physiognomy. Never have I seen such gigantic ears. They are like the overly large ears of desert mice. In fact, as a whole, Waralibi strikingly resembles a mouse. I'm serious. I do no exaggerate.

When Seghers spreads Treml's map out on the sand, Waralibi sniffs at it. Apparently what he sees displeases him, for he takes it in his tiny claws and rips it into a dozen or more pieces. I gasp. Seghers exclaims something in surprise and shock. But Waralibi is reassuring; in a voice that cracks and pitches high, he says, "My stone will show you where to find what you must find."

And that is that. No discussion of our quest other than that Waralibi explains it would take him two days, in consultation with the stone, to help us.

Uneasy, I settle back. I glance at Seghers who meets my eyes and then gestures towards Waralibi and says, "He is a man who knows directions. We must trust him."

And so I resolve to do so. Curious, I ask, "How is it that you two know each other?" What ensues is a difficult to follow narrative which ends with a surprising remark from Seghers: "My friend here was once in love with my sister. With Maeleeva."

I look at Waralibi. The black holes of his eyes seem to glimmer in the firelight. "I still am," he says, showing his front teeth.

Then he asks me about our children. I tell him much. I had noticed earlier that he appeared to want to keep his distance from them. In a dialect I do not recognize, he says, They are *bilorpoliza emka*.

When he does not translate the term, I seek out the face of Seghers.

"It means *things that repulse*," he says. "Monstrosities."

Salmaya, I am angered by the characterization, and yet as Seghers and Waralibi continue talking and explaining the existing views towards deformed children in The Empty Too Much, I begin to control my emotions. Waralibi voices his concerns that many in the realm will desire to kill our children—that doing so would, in their opinion, bring them good fortune. Others might well worship them as having sacred properties, as being holy and deserving of protection. I had heard this kind of thing before.

As we prepare to turn in for the night, I learn that Waralibi—The Listener at the Stone—makes his living through charging caravans to help them locate the correct road or path to their destination. Occasionally, individuals—thrill seekers—would pay him to guide them to *the path no one has found*. He would do so, then abandon them once he had led them there.

Those foolish beings he would never see again.

24

Dearest Salmaya, Soul of My Soul,

In my darker moods, I feel that we are moving into a riddle and a doom.

I feel that in The Empty Too Much the never-believed-in constantly nears.

We stayed two days with The Listener at the Stone. Two days of mystery.

Apparently now confident that he can locate the Gazelle Boy, Seghers curves our trail to the west through very broken country of rock, sand and open, scattered bush; some of the skeletal vegetation sports tiny blue blossoms which he gathers— for what purpose I'm unsure.

My question to him is this: "Did Treml give us a faulty map? Is that why we lost our way?"

"No. I, Seghers, was distracted," he says. "The compass of my heart led me astray."

Was that an allusion to Maeleeva? I wonder.

We lunch on tea and a loaf of flatbread Waralibi sent with us. Our children are quiet. They eat and drink and play with Nightheart's tail. Bloodfire is honking and squawking about who knows what. I honestly would not miss that beast if he were to expire.

I sit and think about the conversation I had with Waralibi on our final night with him. I asked him about monstrosities and what I should expect regarding our children, the likelihood that they could be healed and the dangers they now faced. He seemed not to want to commit himself regarding their being healed, but he held forth on the subject of monstrosities as if he were reading from an encyclopedia devoted to them. Salmaya, never have I heard such detail centering on hairy maidens, stone children, women who lay ostrich-sized eggs, dwarves, giants, hyena men, snake swallowers, conjoined twins, mermaids, horned women and many, many more.

My head swam.

But I'm not certain any of my concerns were assuaged.

During the night I got up to relieve myself and found Waralibi with his small hands pressed upon the remarkable stone as if he were about to heal it of some affliction. Then he rested one ear against it as if he were its confessor.

In the morning, he called Seghers aside and, with a stick, drew a crude map in the sand—the way to the Gazelle Boy? I assumed it was. Seghers traced the outline with his forefinger and nodded.

Then they gestured for me to join them.

I watched as Waralibi sniffed the air for a score of seconds.

Glancing from Seghers to me, he issued a warning: *"Be careful, my friends, there is danger ahead of you and behind you. The one ahead I do not recognize. The one behind I do—be aware that the Hunters are following you."*

Yes, he spoke of those same horrid men who took Nightheart.

Seghers pulled a face of worry and from Waralibi he accepted a fearfully shaped, long knife, curved for violence. It possessed a handle made, it appeared, from the same material as the magical stone.

I could feel my heart speed up and rattle in my chest.

Soberly we said goodbye and set forth.

Out a ways, I looked back.

My final vision of Waralibi was of him lovingly embracing his stone.

25

Dearest Salmaya,

What a perilous day this has been!

On our trek west we found several viable wells. But we skirted villages of superstitious people, those who might discover our children, take them away and murder them.

We came upon an old shepherd who gave us a cup or two of goat's milk for Gela, Simeo and Forg—they were thirsty for it. Their spirits were lifted, even Forg's.

The trouble began around twilight.

I had coaxed life into a fire and was feeding spoons of date paste into the mouths of our children and talking with them about the Gazelle Boy and how much I was counting upon him to help us.

Two things suddenly occurred.

First, Seghers rushed over to Nightheart and Bloodfire and began to chase them away from the campsite.

"What?" I exclaimed.

I looked around for wolves or leopards. I thought of the Hunters, but saw no sign of them.

The second thing was this: Seghers drew the knife Waralibi had given him. He rubbed at the blade of it with his forefinger, then concealed the weapon in his robe.

The gloaming thickened.

And then a figure appeared. A woman—old, thin, ghostly. Veiled, she approached us from the north swaying, dancing without music, or no music that I could hear.

Seghers yelled at me: "Put your children in the tent! Get in there with them!"

"What is it?"

"Do it! Now!"

So I did.

I told our children not to be afraid.

But *I* was.

The woman continued to approach very slowly, weaving and bobbing, her face a mask of mist or smoke, no features clear and discernible except for small, burning red eyes. She wore a gray, tattered shroud—sinister clothing of terror. Then, as I continued looking out through the slit in the tent, I could make out more of her face, including a toothless smile from beyond the grave.

Seghers edged close to the tent.

"It is the Breath Charmer," he said. "A serious threat."

"What does she want?"

He did not answer. Instead, he called out something to the woman.

Momentarily she stopped, but then her dancing increased in pace and frenzy until an extraordinary development occurred: her hands caught on fire. I think that both Seghers and I were stunned as we looked on. When it appeared that her hands were black, charred gloves, her dancing ceased.

And I could smell her breath—fetid and poisonous: the perfume of misery.

I could *see* it. I could see it coiling out from her lips with a serpentine geometry, gray-white and thicker than rope.

Seghers leaned down and whispered, "She can strangle a person with her breath. She can spin a web around one and leave him to die."

And I said again, "What does she want?"

He gestured frantically, saying, "Stay in your tent with your children and do not try to confront her."

I glanced out again at where she stood not more than fifty paces from our campsite.

Her arms writhed and lengthened, ending with the hooded heads of cobras where her blackened hands should have been.

Inside the tent, I surrounded our children, and I quaked.

26

Salmaya, I write in Fear,

The ghastly woman's hissing shattered the night.

"I am the Charmer!" she exclaimed. "I am the Breath of Evil!"

Her eyes, Salmaya—glowing rubies of light, a fire that could not be extinguished.

In our tent, I clutched our children to me and, hearing the voice of that terrifying harpy, they shuddered. Then I could not help myself: inching from my dear ones, I peered through the tent flaps and there was Seghers standing defiantly, his wicked knife drawn, his body braced to protect us.

And suddenly the birds.

What a strange, indescribable sight: a small flock of nameless winged things of falling night, circling the head of the Breath Charmer who merely cackled as they hovered near as threateningly as they could.

But there were not enough of them. They were no match for her.

Lightning quick and shadow silent, her cobra hands struck, claiming one bird after another, tearing their wings from their innocent bodies and needling fangs into their rapidly approaching deaths. The birds screamed for their lives. They thrashed helplessly upon the ground until their hearts were stilled.

It was horrid to see.

The sounds of killing whispered through the calm press of darkness.

Seghers reared up to challenge the consummate cruelty.

But, he, too, was not a strong enough opponent.

I could not bear to watch.

Perhaps a minute of an ensuing, aftermath silence passed before I could summon the courage to see what I could see.

I wish I hadn't.

There, near the dying coals of our fire, Seghers lay, his body cocooned in the white threads of the hideous woman's breath. He did not move. He *could* not move. He looked like an ancient mummy.

The Breath Charmer was nowhere to be seen.

I waited.

How many minutes elapsed I cannot say, but just as I had calculated that I might be able to leave the tent and assist Seghers, Gela tugged at my sleeve and said,

"She has returned."

Yes, it was true.

No more than ten paces from the front of our tent.

We could hear her whispering in the eerie language of Elsewhere.

I knew that we were not imagining her, and that realization shook me with a terror I have never before experienced.

Then the whispering ceased.

The deadly thing beyond our tent was venomously still.

A great, contemplative silence fell around her.

But not for long.

The ultimate terror of her was this: for more than an hour she rocked on her knees in front of our tent, whimpering and keening and whining and calling—yes, *calling*. She was calling our children and that made it even more horrifying than if she had directly attacked. Her voice was unsettling and sad—infinitely sad. Her dark chanting flowed in a language suggestive of melancholy threnodies. It was a voice of eternal sterility; a voice that faded into a deadly nothingness.

Most frightening of all was her breathing.

There was nothing of life that could be lived in it.

I waited, forced to listen to the banshee-like thing cry hideously.

Then, as more minutes passed, I began to hear a new sound. Our children.

As a threesome, they began to mimic the doleful utterances of the Breath Charmer—they were her echo, and in being so I believe they were able to keep the horrors of her from penetrating our tent and overtaking us. I believe, as well, that their knowing attempt helped them to resist her call.

It was a standoff.

But how long could it last?

How strong could our children be?

I doubted their endurance.

Then I braved a glance out and what I saw cheered even as it disturbed me: Nightheart had returned to camp and had gone to Seghers and was biting at the ropes of breath that had bound the man.

The Breath Charmer was unaware, for her attention was given to breaking through the resistance of our children.

Gela's tiny voice drew me to her.

"Dear Father, we are weak. So weak."

Protectively, I threw myself over them even as the pungent breath of the old hag gusted into the tent. I shouted at her, but her presence began quickly to overcome me.

To our children, I whispered, "I love you, three in one. I love you."

Then the horrid woman shrieked, her voice tore, and she was upon us.

27

D earest Salmaya,

Please know that you were with me and our children during those impossible moments. I repeated your name again and again, and the act itself allowed me to stay in a magic circle of sanity and clarity. Your name was like music—the companionship of inner music, your name a holy naming, a symphony of the familiar.

Seghers, released by Nightheart from the evil one's binding, was our rescuer.

Just as the Breath Charmer clutched at us, I heard the sickening thud of that long knife he bore—I heard it drive deeply into her back.

I will never forget the horror of her death thralls.

And I will never forget, as well, the relief I experienced.

A little later as Seghers hurried us into leaving our campsite and the body of the Breath Charmer, I saw, in my thoughts, images of her as a defier of the gods and the mother of all terrors. I realized that even the *smell* of her breath urged suicide. She had stormed the doors of our sanity and our safety. Yet, we had not succumbed to her.

We put a day between us and the memory of her.

But by twilight, our children, dear Salmaya, were deathly weakened. Forg, in fact, muttered of wanting to take his own life. Simeo, ever his good brother, chided him softly, telling him that healing for them was near. "Have patience. Have faith."

Seghers ministered to all three. Maeleeva had given him medicinal seeds of some kind, and these he gave to our children in large doses. Almost instantly, they fell asleep as children do in fairy tales.

At our night fire, I thanked Seghers as we drank our tea.

"Maeleeva deserves those words, not me," he said. "Her medicine will work for a day or two. They must get strong on their own."

"You must care deeply for your sister," I said.

He nodded, but said nothing for several minutes. Then he shifted his body and stared up at the heavens.

"She knows the sacred cosmogony of Piro Seghers. No one else does. No one else can."

While I did not fully comprehend, I was pleased that he shared his thoughts.

And so we turned away from each other to rest and recover from the ordeal of the Breath Charmer. We had slept perhaps two hours when both of us were awakened by the sound of birds in the near distance. They were agitated.

Seghers stood and looked towards the north and west.

I heard him murmur, "No, please. No."

Alarmed, I stumbled to his side.

"What is it?" I exclaimed.

And there she was—her ghost, that is. The Breath Charmer. She had returned.

And her voice was on fire.

His long knife in hand, Seghers braced himself for another fight. For my part, I picked up two rocks large enough to do some damage to one not a ghost , but, oh, Salmaya, I am not ashamed to say that I was, once again, terrified.

She approached from deep shadows.

She moved or glided without taking steps.

I saw the hand of Seghers quiver.

And then we heard the birds again, a raging cacophony of them.

And then we looked upon a most bizarre scene: those birds—hundreds or even thousands of them—descended upon the ghost of the Breath Charmer, her living dead, almost alive corpse—and covered her with a sinister feathering and vengeful screeching until her shrieking was completely muted.

After a number of riveting minutes, the birds all at once took flight.

And nothing remained of our nemesis.

Nothing except harmless wisps of her ghostly breath, gray and lacking luster, like death itself.

28

Salmaya, Companion of My Thoughts,

This morning our children are better. While they are not hungry, they are thirsty, and they are jabbering among themselves as if private noises will help them slough off recent horrors. I tell them that the Breath Charmer is no longer a threat to us. I'm not certain that they believe me.

Our children and I took special pains to thank Nightheart for his heroic action in freeing Seghers. That wonderful creature nosed at them, sensing, I believe, that they had suffered and that they needed more strength. Seghers tried to reward Nightheart when he could, providing him with young thistle sprouts that grow near the rock formations and in rills not yet completely dry. Unfortunately, Bloodfire remained his stubborn, increasingly uncooperative self. But we needed him, and Seghers no longer beat him as much.

Before the sun baked our trail too much, we were treated to the sight of a train of a half dozen or more desert elephants crossing in front of us; they marched purposefully as if they had an appointment at the end of the realm. I see such mystery in their gray visages—they combine grace and power. They enchant me and our children. At the sight of them, Seghers said, "Can you feel their ancient life force?"

Yes. Yes, we could.

Just past our lunch stop, we saw a band of *ftez* less than a quarter of a mile away. Seghers did not seem particularly glad to see them. Perhaps the Breath Charmer had made him wary, or perhaps he didn't want any kind of distraction that might cause us to once again lose our way.

Ftez are women. The Barrens. Sisters of the Barren.

Outcasts because they cannot bare children. They travel together alone.

This particular group had around ten in it. Seghers explained that typically a collection of them would have women ranging in age from teenagers to the quite old. In The Empty Too Much, such women are thought to be *xopinsteri* or demonic spirits; it is also thought that they possess *omumwa*—a capacity for employing the Evil Eye.

For several hours, they walked parallel to our track, edging close enough for me to make out that most were wearing rags and had urine-colored, lifeless hair. Seghers warned me to avoid making eye contact with them—to just ignore them and, likely, they would not pose a threat.

"Do the children draw their interest?" I asked.

"Yes, but they know who I am. I doubt that they will bother us."

Evening arrived. We built our fire. I played Grinner for our children. Gela and Simeo sang. Seghers smoked and thumbed through his old, thick book. A cool breeze from the south kicked up, and from that direction we heard the surreal yips of wild dogs and the nonsense laughter of hyenas.

And then the Barrens began songs of their own.

Oh, Salmaya, now I better understand that mystery is part of beauty.

The Barrens—sirens of the oncoming night. Of what did they sing? I sensed that they were lamenting their sterile wombs and their claw-like hands. As they continued singing and chanting, they approached to within fifty or sixty paces of our camp, and they gathered faggots as if to start a fire. I glanced at Seghers, but his face had a sanguine cast to it, so I was not afraid.

Our children scuttled to my side. They wished to view these strange women.

I listened more intently, and I realized that the Barrens could not help it if their laments sounded so beautiful, so ethereal. I saw each one of them more clearly then. They sang out of their vacant, childless faces with individual modulations woven together into a rope of sound so fiercely strong that nothing could fray it—or so I imagined. The beauty of it bound me, yet not like the danger of the Breath Charmer; Gela and Simeo hummed along with the production, and Forg parted his lips in awe, I believe.

I noticed suddenly that two of the women were cradling small children. When I pointed this out to Seghers he shook his head and explained that often with their claw-like hands they will dig up dead children and mother them and that on occasion, the more violent and crazed members of the tribe have been known to rip babies from the wombs of pregnant women—such members are immediately exiled. Some are stoned to death.

I winced at his words, and I tensed when their lamenting softened to where it was nearly inaudible like the indifferent murmuring of flowing water—a distant purling. When the Barrens saw our children, they asked Seghers whether they could come closer. I told him that they could.

They crept forward another fifteen or twenty paces and there they piled their faggots and started a small fire. Reflections from the flames dancing in their eyes, not repulsed, they stared at our children: they didn't touch; they adored, and it reminded me of paintings I have seen of men and women adoring god-like children.

Then, Salmaya, a most arresting spectacle.

As their fire rose higher, they began a new chant. I saw that they had singled out one young tribe member, barely more than a girl, her face almost hopeful; she placed herself closer to the flames; she sat akimbo and waited.

Soon, from the center of the fire, embers heaved as if something living had burrowed there and was seeking escape. The chanting of the Barrens thickened and then spiraled up in a glorious lilt until it became at first a small, shapeless entity and began to levitate out of the embers.

Salmaya, it soon evidenced that it was the form a child.

A burning infant.

Birthed from the fiery embers, it sought the arms of the waiting woman.

And though it burned her flesh and her clothing, she took the child and hugged it to her breasts and to it she began to sing a lullaby.

The ritualistic scene brought tears to my eyes as well as to the eyes of our children. Even Seghers appeared to be moved.

And then the night came to an end.

The Barrens put out their fire and drifted slowly away like smoke.

As if they did not, in fact, exist.

29

Dearest Salmaya,

The Barrens returned the next morning.

We greeted them. We offered them food and water, but they politely refused.

Then they sang for us a *spajeneno*—a good journey song, and a good wishes chant as well. Seghers explained that in the chant they had embedded a reference to The People of the Wild.

"What is their view of those people?" I said to him.

"They reverence them. They speak of them as those who protect those who cannot protect themselves."

When their songs and chants ended, we thanked them, but before they went on their way Seghers asked whether they had recently seen the Gazelle Boy. "Where may one find him?" he said.

Several of the women immediately pointed west towards a pair of extinct volcanic cones, rugged and daunting because of their height.

One more thing: as the Barrens were leaving, Gela and Simeo began their own song in that secret language they have. I could tell that it pleased the women; one, in fact, approached a few steps and, with tears streaming down her face, bowed her head and rocked forward again and again; then, in that same secret tongue of our children, she wailed words that I chose to interpret as blessings.

30

Dearest Salmaya,

More and more I realize that these are letters from the silence you gave birth to. Thank you for, each day, making your strength and your love a living presence to me and our children.

We travel on.

We pass through abandoned days and abandoned villages.

The landscape, a mix of black lava stone and sand, loses monotony at times when we enter salt depressions and areas of stunted palms. Here and there we find a cool water well, deep and dark; elsewhere, the closer we get to the massive volcanic cones the more frequently we come upon hot springs where our children enjoy bathing. They continue to find long stretches of time in which to hold Maeleeva's small, round stones in their mouth. They are trying to help themselves; even Forg, somewhat. It's a heartache on days when their battle against the approach of death appears to lose ground.

One night recently, with our children nearing sleep, I made a special effort to sit up with Seghers. I sensed that we might not be far from our destination—from the promise of the Gazelle Boy. The flames of our timid fire sighed as if contented or bored—who could tell which? Seghers, squatting on his heels, murmured aloud, "There is an old saying in The Empty Too Much: The inner side of the wind is the one that remains dry when the wind blows through the rain." Finishing his remark, he gazed into the fire as if studying his reflection in a mirror.

I yawned.

I was pleased that our children, restless and feverish most

of the day, had settled in; it was not long before under the black cloth their snoring was, I believed, a continuous reassurance to them.

"It's always about the wind, isn't it, old man?" I said. "Or the sand. Or the stars. Or the night." I glanced over to make certain Seghers understood that no mean spiritedness flowed through my words.

"And mirages," said Seghers, "if one knows how to read them."

At the rim that spread away from us, where shadow and light partnered, Nightheart stood with his head bowed thoughtfully; Bloodfire, eyes closed, knelt, but shifted his camel bones now and again as if searching for a comfortable position.

"You're always reading something out there," I added. "The desert is your book."

"Not true, young man." He slipped the comically tattered volume from somewhere within his robe. "I am a man of letters as well as a man of wind, sand and stars."

I sensed that an opportunity had presented itself.

"What is your big poem about?"

Seghers knew by now that I had spoken with Maeleeva about his dedicated task, and yet he appeared surprised by my question. Quickly he recovered himself.

"Of men and wounds," he said. "And loss." He held the old book lovingly, thumbing its pages, then frowning. He seemed to be weighing something, something perhaps more valuable than gold. Then he said, "It's about how men are wounded by the invisible."

The line momentarily expunged my thoughts. Not confusion. It was a more complete, deeper effect than that. I rose to check on our children. When I adjusted the way Simeo's hand was jammed under his chin, the boy farted softly. I smiled, kissed his head and returned to my spot by the fire.

To my companion I said, "I could only write a poem about how much I still love my wife and how much I love my children and want them to be healed."

Seghers had lighted a cigarette. He squinted through spirals of smoke.

"Have you never heard that love is a wound?" he said.
I felt my senses ruffle: "Isn't that the sentiment of silly, overly romantic poetry?" I replied.

Raising one finger in a declarative gesture, he shook his head very slowly and for quite some moments before he spoke.

"Not if the poet loves his wound and lives only to praise it."

That word *praise*—he had emphasized it before.

His declaration bled mystery. I found no way to counter it.

31

My Beautiful Salmaya,

Oh, the gods have smiled!

But when I woke this morning, I believed that they had abandoned us. Imagine the rush of panic I felt when upon emerging from our tent, I glanced around and saw that Seghers and Nightheart and Bloodfire were not around.

My heart beat in my throat.

I jogged out into the muted gold of first light and called out for Seghers. Where on earth could he be? Why had he taken both Nightheart and Bloodfire? My calls volleyed eerily between the two volcanic cones.

Had we been left behind?

Had Seghers succumbed to madness?

I had no idea.

Unfortunately, our children woke earlier than usual. I went about building our breakfast fire as if nothing unusual had occurred. Alas, I wasn't skilled at hiding my anxieties.

"Dear Father, Dear Father," said Gela, "where are the others?"

"Well, oh, … well, you see, I think they have gone for water."

Simeo smelled my deception.

"Are we lost again?"

Forg grunted angrily. And so I hunkered down close to our children and spoke softly—and this time truthfully—that I did not know where Seghers had gone but that we must trust him.

"Dear Father," said Gela, "we'll sing for his safe return." A haunting hymn rose from the lips of Gela and Simeo. As usual,

I could not understand their words. Forg whimpered like a forsaken puppy.

I went about fixing porridge.

The sun painted the sides of the volcanic cones with a patina of red-orange. I heard the distant sniggle of a hyena. High in the sky desert vultures circled listlessly. We ate our breakfast. We waited.

When it was approaching noon, I thought maybe I was hearing things, for the distinct whinny of Nightheart echoed, bouncing between the cones. I shaded my eyes against the hammer of the sun and there—there moving down an almost invisible path of one of the cones was Seghers and Nightheart and Bloodfire. I was of a sudden deeply thankful.

Then an unreasonable anger seized me.

When the three of them reached our camp, I cursed Seghers and questioned him, giving him no chance, at first, to explain. I was shaking with dismay and fear.

But there was calm in his manner and carriage. He put a hand on my shoulder and said, "Wait a little longer. Have courage. Tell your children to believe. Only believe."

"Is the Gazelle Boy coming?" I said.

He turned then to cast his eyes at the cone on the left, at the fluting on its hard surface, the pattern of it resembling the melting of a giant candle. I glanced at it, too, and found it difficult not to be in awe of how the cone rose to seemingly improbable heights.

Seghers shook his head. "Believe. Just believe."

Then, late afternoon, our having suffered through hours of anguished waiting, Seghers issued a bird-like cry and pointed at the cone.

There.

Two figures.

A human and an animal. Moving slowly, with an ease and confidence most impressive, two living things descended as naturally as if they belonged to the ancient volcano.

I positioned our children so that they could view the event.

I heard them purring; I heard them praying deep in their throats.

Even Forg.

Oh, Salmaya!

As the exhausted sun began to release its hold on the day, the Gazelle Boy simply walked off the steep formation of the volcano right into our camp—he and his lovely, delicate gazelle.

I fell to my knees at their approach.

The Gazelle Boy: a very young man—could he have been sixteen years of age?—wearing a saffron-colored loincloth and dusty sandals with an adorable, mystical face and large, brown, almond-shaped eyes (that matched those of his gazelle), stepped among us. Two small horns pointed backwards from either side of his head; his face and naked chest and arms and legs were very tanned and his hair was the blackest I have ever seen.

Seghers bowed to him as if he were royalty.

Our children cooed like doves.

The gazelle itself, prancing on hooves that appeared to be as fragile as glass, stayed close to the side of the young man. It was a beautiful, beautiful creature.

The Gazelle Boy walked up to where I knelt.

He tilted his head as if merely curious.

Then he smiled.

Salmaya, I nearly fainted with relief.

I nearly cried with joy.

32

Salmaya, My Love,

Seghers says this of the Gazelle Boy: "He has learned the long truth about the boundaries between what is great and what is small."

I cannot doubt those words.

That first night I stayed up late, dozing off and on as an inspired oneiric wind blew from the west. What dreams were delivered to me? Fragmented ones—yet, they were pieces of everything good that I have ever experienced—such as our love, Salmaya, and our children and peaceful, untroubled days in The Land of Speaking Rivers.

But I must try now to capture some sense of what it is like to have the Gazelle Boy, whose name is *Good Face*, and his gazelle—the creature is known as *Dune*—among us. I can only begin by saying that when I watch Good Face and Dune with our children I seem to enter a sacred space where I have no right to be. I am a trespasser. An outsider.

I want to shout: Remember! These are my children! My flesh and blood!

Because I feel protective and frightened and so hopeful, I often tremble within. Of course, I say nothing. I must trust and believe. In incomprehensible ways, our children now belong to The Empty Too Much and the healing forces it has given birth to.

I feel bewitched. Like something chilled and harrowed and solemn.

I live and breathe in the heart of stillness.

At the request of Good Face, we have moved our camp to the base of one of the volcanic cones. There we are sheltered by a dark outcropping of lava rock, and we are shaded from the sun. And there Good Face and Dune sit with our children and Good Face speaks their language and forges a bond I cannot possibly imagine. He touches each of them tenderly, and then, in turn, invites them to touch Dune, to pet him and get to know him. They all appear to be the best of friends.

Is this a phase of the healing process?

There is magic afoot—of that I am certain.

For example, I looked on at one point as Good Face asked each of our children to give him the small stone they had received from Maeleeva. He took the three stones and clasped them in his palm; he closed his eyes and appeared to shudder. He squeezed hard. And when he opened his hand … yes, the three stones had become one larger stone. Then he directed them to pass the stone from one to the other; they did so, giggling, happy—even Forg. Then he explained that, whenever they experienced doubt or fear, they should share the stone, passing it and keeping contact with good fortune.

I have also witnessed the following: when a strong wind batters our site, Good Face will, at times, choose to stand and raise his hand, palm out as if pushing back at the natural force. At that point, Salmaya, the wind ceases. It dies away. How to explain it? I do not know. And there is also something magical about Dune—his incarnate beauty, unity of soul and form, his open attentiveness to whatever may break into the desert's magic circle in which the five of them exist.

I've noticed that Seghers spends more time at twilight and again at dawn secreting himself away from our camp where, I believe, he listens to what the invisible gods dictate. I study his reaction. I sense that some of what he hears upsets him, yet he hides his emotions well.

Mystery upon mystery grows here where virtually nothing else does.

My beautiful Salmaya, I wish you were here in the flesh.

I need your strength.

Help me to trust what is difficult.

Help me to embrace the inscrutable possibilities of life in The Empty Too Much.

33

Dearest Salmaya,

This morning at dawn Seghers said to me, "If you let this light fill you, you will be capable of doing something remarkable."

He might be right, of course, but I seem to have so much darkness within that light can barely enter. The sky of my inner realm is a black seething of questions. Pieces of undigested shame roil in my stomach.

Why must I doubt?

Why must I fear?

Would that courage might tumble from the far side of the universe like a meteorite and strike me like an answer from the beyond.

As I sat at our morning fire wallowing in self-pity, Dune approached from behind and gently nudged me. His magnificent eyes asked me questions. Or maybe those eyes were saying to me: *There are no answers.*

I have written off my anguish as a simple case of jealousy.

At the core of my doubts and fears coils a reptilian envy of the relationship of Good Face and Dune with our children. If I could smite that viper with my heel, I would do it. I truly would.

After breakfast and a second cup of tea, a stranger entered camp. Good Face, pleased to see the visitor, explained that he was a *zeproal*, a singer of threnodies of detachment and departure. But, oh, Salmaya, what a bizarre figure he was: short and squat and very black and bearded; his arms were quite hairy and his bare toes were connected by thin, iron nails that must have been painfully driven through them. I was timid about shaking hands with him. Seghers appeared to know him, for the two embraced in desert style.

The *zeproal*—who remained nameless—smiled at our children; he allowed them—in fact, encouraged them—to touch his beard and his hairy arms. The only thing he brought with him was a rather long, boxy-shaped 12-string instrument. We all looked on as he seated himself before our children and began to sing and pluck the weird instrument.

Seghers, sensing my puzzlement, whispered to me, "He's singing the death of your children's affliction. An elegy to the Wasting."

I had never heard music quite like it.

It was as if it had been composed on a different planet.

At the end of the man's nearly hour long performance, our children softly applauded. Good Face stepped forward and asked the *zeproal* to sing one more song.

And this one, my Salmaya, was even more beautiful than the one directed to our children. As the strings of the instrument called out, and as magical words slipped from the tongue of the *zeproal*, I turned to Seghers who seemed to be deeply enchanted.

"It is a familiar song," he said. "It is known as *Ode To The People of the Wild.*"

But I could not understand the words.

"What is the message of the song?" I asked.

Seghers paused for a quite a long spell as if considering the best way to respond. At last he said, "It is a song of praise—a song to thank the gods for allowing such mystical people to exist."

Then the *zeproal* kissed each of our children on the cheek and muttered some kind of a blessing, I believe. And, seconds later, he departed. He seemed, indeed, to shiver out of sight like a figure caught in a mirage. Wind and sand and heat dissolved him into a moment of soundless invisibility.

The ode played in my thoughts the rest of the day.

Night came on, and a nearly full moon rose.

I hugged our children.

Good Face touched my shoulder, a gesture at once reassuring

and mysterious. I made myself a pallet next to the fire and soon fell asleep.

Long after midnight I woke with a stab of alarm.

I cried out until Seghers virtually wrestled me to the ground.

They were gone, Salmaya!

Good Face and Dune and our children!

They disappeared as completely as if I had dreamed up each one of them.

34

Dearest Salmaya,

I am somewhat calmer this morning.

Seghers helped me through the night. He made me smoke one of his hallucinogenic cigarettes. In response to it, I swam in a sea of stars among bright yellow fishes. Then I flew through rock and dived down into the bowels of The Empty Too Much and walked across burning lava flows laughing and singing.

When the hallucination finally relented, Seghers spoke loudly and very close to my face: "This is his way," he said. "This must be. It's his way."

But my worries nearly crushed me.

I trembled with the realization that I must trust the process that was ongoing. Seghers reminded me that the Gazelle Boy felt confident he could heal our children—all three of them.

"Hold a picture in your thoughts," said Seghers, "of the three of them running, hearts filled with poetry, living without rejecting anything of the thankless desert, anything of life itself."

I appreciated his elegantly worded advice.

But when I continued to mope, he said, "Tomorrow we shall go to the *images*."

When he would not explain what he meant, I walked out away from our campsite at twilight. Oh, Salmaya, a silent desert is a merciless thing. I stayed several hundred paces from our fire; I allowed the end of day to surround me. I had wicked, ugly thoughts: I imagined an adolescent night copulating with darkness, an old hag. I stood alone and felt demonic spirits released out there by the wind—or riding upon it—sensed them piercing and biting and poisoning the air.

I found that I could not breathe.

After midnight, Nightheart came for me. Did Seghers send him? I assume he did, but then again that remarkable wild ass is more than human in his compassion and generosity.

I collapsed onto my pallet.

Seeking oblivion, I slept instead the sleep of despair.

At dawn, Seghers handed me a bitter cup of strong tea and made me drink it down. He grinned knowingly and said, "The skulls went home?"

How could he have known?

Yes, that was my nightmare: bodiless skulls dancing, jabbering about me as a black sand clotted with icy particles blew through my skin and lodged within. The skulls, hideous companions, wandered with me through the landscape of my inner being as I sought to find something worth finding.

The night of the skulls.

"Yes," I said, "and I pray that they will stay there—wherever it is."

It was then I took up my quill and began writing these words to you. Although he had many times noticed me writing, Seghers finally took the opportunity to ask about my task.

"What are you writing?"

Perhaps too rashly I responded, "Letters to a dead woman who lives in my heart."

I blushed with a curious embarrassment. I hated the sound of the words *dead woman*—I ask that you forgive me.

"Your wife, I assume. Is she … do you believe she is in the *beyond*? In the *afterlife*?"

"No," I said. "I mean, I have no such belief and neither did she. But, of course, I don't know. I just don't know. I feel her spirit. I sense something of her, and so do our children."

For a long stretch of seconds, Seghers did not speak. Uncomfortable with his silence, I explained that you, Salmaya, and I have always believed in *goodness*, in something innate that could never partake of cruelty. I explained that in The Land of Speaking Rivers many shared that basic mindset. We embraced no dogma. We claimed no corner on the truth.

"What about you?" I said. "Those voices that dictate to you—those gods of the invisible—are they *divine*?"

"I think so," he muttered.

Then, in a rambling, at times incoherent confession, he spoke of the divine as something infinitely distant, unattainable. Something demanding that we search ourselves for at the root of our being.

Then he shook himself as if he had been in a trance and said, "In The Empty Too Much, it is claimed that men and women are not born to breathe the same air as the divine."

"I just don't know," I said again.

Seghers nodded.

"Let us talk of these things another day. The *images* await us."

35

Salmaya, Dear Love,

The stillness around us cries out to be filled with something vast. The stunned rubble of morning promises a day infested with things glistening and threatening—things I cannot identify. I look up. The high desert sky, a terrible mirror, has been cracked by the wing tips of black vultures. I do not want to leave our camp for fear that the Gazelle Boy and our children will return and wonder where we are. Seghers assures me that it is not time for them to come. To be patient.

We strike off south towards a wall of rock peppered with caves.

We say little to each other. The space between our responses draws us into emptiness. At times I sense that I am sleepwalking through the bright day, negotiating between what I fear I have lost and what I am learning how to recover. Rough poetry hums in my ear: streams of anxiety flow into lakes of bottomless madness.

I have been sentenced to live in circles of memory.

We stop in a thorn tree grove to tend to our thirst.

And it suddenly occurs to me that away from sizable villages in The Empty Too Much there is little law, few if any enforcement officials; the potential for uncivil acts to be committed is great, and the potential for savagery is greater even than the number and intensity of mirages.

Seghers wipes his lips and reties his water cask.

"The past sheds light but never keeps us warm," he says.

I counter with, "The heart is what must keep us warm."

Seghers wags his eyebrows as if amused.

"Is there not a dungeon somewhere deep in one's heart?"

I admit that he might be right, but my thoughts have already sped off in a different direction.

"I want only to escape that kind of place and experience the future. I long for a darkness I can read the pages of tomorrow by."

"Yes," says Seghers, "but you must accept both the bounty and the hostility of tomorrow. You won't be allowed to edit those pages."

I nod acceptance.

In another two hours, we gain the foot of the rock wall. Scanning it as if he is remembering something, Seghers clears his throat.

Prepare to be astonished.

Oh, Salmaya, he knew. He knew.

One hundred feet or so up a meandering, rocky path we came to the mouth of a large cave. I glanced down to where we had left Nightheart and Bloodfire and my stomach filled with cold air. A wave of curious anticipation staggered me, and I asked myself, *What wants to come?* More so, from some dark, inaccessible corner of my mind a voice issued forth: *When the gods have filled you with fullness, your Fate will disappear.*

Salmaya, what could that mean?

Then Seghers ignited a torch, and we entered the darkness where figures chalked on the rock walls emitted the glare of revelations. While I can't begin to name all that we saw, I will try to summarize a marvelous flood of images. They included the following: giant buffalo, giraffes, cattle, camels, crocodiles, elephants, leopards, goats and cheetahs. Humans, too—one large panel of men with bows, arrows and spears hunting and, as well, dancing as if in triumph. There were also extremely thin men and women fornicating and a strange, small depiction of women in their time of the month with a black demon catching their blood in a cup. Can you believe it?

There were images of dog-headed men and of cheetah women frozen in transformation from human to animal and back again. There was even a stunning depiction of what I believe was a Man of Never, a vile and monstrous creature, and a clustered flow of black, eyeless figures with stubby arms and web-like tails instead of legs and feet. Although they seemed sexless, I felt they resembled mermaids.

"What are these?" I said.

I was much surprised when he murmured, "The People of the Wild."

I stared at them in awe, and then I said, "They appear to be swimming—swimming deep in a lake or a sea."

Seghers dismissed my observation. "No, he said, they are traversing the realm of oblivion, a realm of their own. It is said that they themselves created the realm."

"Where does it lie?"

"It is said that if it exists, it must be buried in The Black Mountains."

Salmaya, I tried to drink in all of the information; I tried to catalogue it for later. I was amazed.

Other extraordinary images awaited me as Seghers led me farther into the cave, into a region we reached only after crawling many, many feet through a narrow shaft. Our path ended abruptly at the edge of a small pool of water only a few paces across.

But then Seghers lifted his torch and blazed it along the wall beyond the pool.

Goodness alive, Salmaya, what I saw!

Depictions of trimanoids.

Six or seven, and if I recall correctly, each about the size of my hand. Each so boldly resembling our children that I gasped aloud at the sight of them. When I glanced at Seghers, his eyes shone with an understanding I did not think he was capable of. I stammered out one word: *Wondrous!* Then I tonelessly repeated it several times. I felt as if a dozen hearts were beating inside my chest.

What followed astonished me beyond words.

Far beyond.

Seghers gently grasped my shoulder and murmured, "You must wade into the pool. Wade into it, and you will know what you otherwise could never possibly know."

In the torchlight, I searched his expression.

Confused, puzzled, I said, "How deep is it?"

Seghers merely shook his head. Again, he exhorted me to enter the pool.

As I slipped off my sandals, for some reason I thought of our children. I did not, in the slightest, know what to expect. Standing upon the edge of the pool, I must admit that I quivered.

The surface of the impossibly black water was cold, and yet as I moved into it and it rose to my waist it became quite warm—a soothing, relaxing warmth like nothing I have ever experienced. Then I heard the voice of Seghers.

"Let the images enter you. Open yourself to them."

With a good bit of timidity, I closed my eyes, took a deep breath.

And in a matter of seconds, my common, every day sense of self disappeared.

Vanished.

Replaced by what? you ask.

Something astonishing.

Please hear this, Salmaya, for a minute or more, there in that mysterious pool far into that nameless cave, there were *three of me*. Joined at the spine, the three of us became aware of each other.

Salmaya, I touched their hands.

I swear that I did.

And I heard them speak softly. They seemed to know me.

But then, very suddenly, the illusion—if that's what it was—faded, and it did so because I cried out, not in pain; rather, it was as if I had been seized by a life-threatening consternation.

The words I exclaimed into the partial darkness?

"Who am I?"

36

Dear Salmaya, Ghost of My Temporal Life,

That night, back at our campsite, I so longed to see our children. I wanted to share with them the galvanizing ecstasy of the cave pool and its transformational insights. I wanted to tell them that I knew. I *knew*.

Seghers and I gnawed on dried, roasted goat meat. We drank strong tea. I had been shaken by the art on the walls of the cave. I had been taken out of myself by the three-in-one sensations of self: the *I* of me as trimanoid, as monstrosity.

Like our children.

Seghers sensed that I had received answers to questions I had not asked and that the cave had given birth to new questions impossible to answer. He spoke into the falling of night as if he were addressing agents of the invisible.

"The voices of The Empty Too Much," he said, "have shapes not yet fully themselves."

I chuckled under my breath. It was my signal to him that I saw reality as being stranger than fantasy or illusions or his cryptic words. He continued, delivering what I characterized in my thoughts as one of his *fire sermons*—the flicker of flames releasing him into an autonomous speech pattern. Along the way I stopped listening: a mysterious feeling began to crawl across the darkened desert towards me. I imagined it as an insect, one I'd never *truly* seen. It resonated with the quiet, oh so quiet sound of a spider spinning a web. And the image set me to thinking of how eager, so very eager I was to see our children *healed*—no longer multi-legged, *released* to be unique individuals, even Forg.

Because of the cave pool experience, I understood that life is mostly about the *body*. The *body* is our most trustworthy contact with reality; furthermore, the flames of our small fire reminded me that in moments of alarm each breath is an angry little victory over death. One's heart beats, clean and hungry, for the promise of blood continuing to flow.

37

Salmaya, Whose Understanding Passes All,

Sometimes the wind staggers like a drunkard.

And so it did as we woke the next morning. But, of course, Seghers seems never truly concerned about or fearful of the wind. I should say *winds*, for there are many of them. Seghers knows each of them intimately—knows the emotional texture of each, knows where it was birthed, knows its color, its taste and smell. He lets certain winds embrace him like a lover. Knows which ones are evil, knows which bring madness. Above all, he knows that the various winds of The Empty Too Much harbor otherness, that each is as full of mystery as water or blood.

Seghers intruded upon my thoughts as if he'd been listening to my musings: "This realm," he said, "possesses unharnessed forces."

And thus, choked with dirty, heat-haze mirages another day was upon us.

That pack of cheetahs we had seen once before approached us warily from the north treading with their patient, ethereal grace. Then, all but one turned and swung in a gentle arc some distance from us. Rising to acknowledge the bold one slinking our way, Seghers lifted one arm and called out, "*Beszneki,Tovelmi. Beszneki.*"

He was welcoming the beautiful cat.

And then, in no more than three or four blinks of an eye, the animal dissolved. A young woman, in a robe the color of the sun, occupied the same space and stepped to within ten or fifteen paces of us. Oh, Salmaya, she was lovely, perhaps no more than twenty years old, slender with magnificently green eyes apparent to me even at a distant. She repeated the name *Seghers* several times.

Her voice… It pattered like a soft rain. It trickled into my ears. There was a nakedness about her embrace of the landscape. Her transformation from swift feline to young woman had been like a prayer to the sky, her arresting beauty like a continuous amen.

When she neared, Seghers introduced us. While she did not offer her hand, I felt somehow as if she had touched me, physically as well as spiritually.

Tovelmi, I whispered. Then I turned to Seghers: "What does her name mean?"

Seghers said he did not know.

I call her, he said, smiling at her animal-like elegance, *"The Girl With Eyes of the Wind."*

I was deeply moved.

She explained that she could not stay. Seghers told her of our children and of the healing process being orchestrated by the Gazelle Boy. She seemed already aware of the fact. To me she spoke with notes of hope that the healing would be successful. I thanked her.

Forgive me, Salmaya, but I knew I would not easily forget her.

Later in the day, as Seghers guided me towards the village of Tir—the original home of the Gazelle Boy—I saw a cheetah sitting upon a small dune not far away looking at us. Looking at me. Then a shift. And there she was again, a young woman peering into the very heart of who I was and at all I longed for in my life.

Tovelmi. The Girl With Eyes of the Wind.

Then she turned and began to lope away, shedding the woman she was, streaming into an animal that seemed capable of outrunning the wind.

An hour passed before we began to cross The Plain of Nothingness. It is a low, flat area flowing out from a maze of windblown dunes and bordered on the east by the brilliant whiteness of salt sediment. Before we trekked through it, Seghers suggested that I take a swig of his blue wine to protect against *bninuou entn*, the affliction of nothingness, the chief effect of which is to make one imagine that he no longer exists.

Bloodfire balked at moments, but otherwise Nightheart, Seghers and I negotiated the hostile plain and soon approached the village of Tir perched upon a shelf of rock and sand, treeless and completely exposed to the sun.

Salmaya, it was a most strange village.

I must apologize for sharing some of its hideousness, but I feel that I should in order for you to understand what it can be like to journey through The Empty Too Much.

Low, white-washed stone buildings make up much of the village. It is a dust-filled place reeking of death—and its inhabitants are largely freaks and mutants and monstrosities. A particularly sorrowful enterprise greets one near the entrance to the village: The Palace of Dead Hearts. Certainly *not* a palace! Rather it is a dark, smelly establishment with a vile gash of blackness for a door.

"What is on sale there?" I said to Seghers.

He shook his head gravely and spit out a single word: "Perversion."

Of course, I pressed him for details.

I soon wished that I had not, for he told me that in the confines of that opprobrious den sex-starved men could buy time with a woman. I was not in the least shaken by that; however, then he added, "Dead women. Relations are with lifeless bodies. *Infernality.*"

I was speechless.

Then he guided me to where we would meet the mother of the Gazelle Boy—The House of Dissection. There women known as Corpse Washers busied themselves as if merely doing their laundry while others engaged in the revolting work of slicing into naked chests and bellies, believing that the act of dissection carried with it the possibility of re-animating the dead person.

I did not watch closely.

In one corner of the large dissection and corpse washing area was a woman known as *Ngeza*, the mother of the Gazelle Boy. When Seghers introduced me to her she was busy tending to an obscenely heavy woman who—it was claimed—had recently given birth to a desert antelope.

I thanked Ngeza for her generosity regarding our children. Her face had been eaten upon by a gnawing sorrow, something unspeakable she had suffered or perhaps was about to suffer. Her expression carried an agonized penitence without hope. She was, in sum, the saddest human being I have ever met. Her words to me? Tearfully, she told me that she pitied me, but did not elaborate. My attention, in fact, had been stolen by the sight of the fascinating, crumpled horn, like that of a mountain goat, plunging downward from her forehead and dangling there between her eyes. She was pale and very thin. I wanted to hug away the deformity of her presence. As tenderly as possible, I touched the back of her hand: it was as cold as ice.

I felt a strangled urge to embrace sunlight.

When we left The House of Dissection, we were converged upon by a menagerie almost unimaginable: a hog-faced woman, a dozen or more dwarves, a giant, a tall, thin man who swallowed live snakes, all manner of cripples and those either missing limbs or possessing extra ones, and a young, frightened-looking woman whose body was completely covered in dark, reddish hair.

We fought our way through them, and I begged Seghers to take me back to our campsite. It was, Salmaya, an indescribable relief to sit by our fire and drink tea. But when I glanced up at the night sky I experienced wild storms of stardust, and I heard hollow, silent voices calling me.

Seghers understood my discomfort. He offered me one of his cigarettes, urging that I smoke it to ward off nightmares. Foolishly, I turned it down. And that night I dreamed that I saw our three children dying, their almost dead faces opening like blood-colored flowers near me, yet not close enough to touch.

38

Salmaya, Salmaya!

I woke in a silence so profound that the breeze against my ears was like a child's sleepy whisper; in fact, I sensed that our children were trying to tell me something—perhaps to prepare me for something.

When Seghers woke, he seemed very sober. Worry tracked across his brow. He paused over his first cup of tea in which he had spooned goat's milk and said, "What's best for man is never to be born."

Ironically, we then launched into a discussion of grief and loss and the universality of suffering, and we agreed that suffering was very much like the wind: a fundamental condition of life. And I recalled what you, Salmaya, said to me once: "We must all bear loss, no matter whom we love." I shared those words with Seghers.

He nodded. He sniffed the air.

"The Hunters have moved through," he said.

I ignored him, for I was suddenly awash in negative memories of Tir. The village had sickened me; the experience of it beat at my senses, bloodied me, leaving me with only one wish—to see our children again, to hold them and to give them my love. I did not even think about whether their condition had been healed.

Before mid-morning arrived, a scorching wind kicked up. Seghers tasted it and declared that out not far into that oblivion of rock and desert a locust breeding ground had developed. He said that we must avoid it. Before I could ask him to explain, we were assaulted by a blinding storm of sand and salty dust with some particles being tiny, blackened basalt shards. We protected our eyes. We weathered the attack.

And then we heard the eerie, distress-filled whinny of Nightheart.

Seghers, obviously alarmed, stood like a statue.

"Ah, the gods, the gods! I greatly feared this!" he exclaimed.

I chased after him as he ran to calm the frightened animal whose fear had also infected Bloodfire.

"What is it?" I called out. "Tell me what's wrong?"

Staring up at one of the volcanic cones, Seghers seemed, for a few moments, to be meditating. He said nothing. He looped a rope over the neck of Nightheart and hurried away, wordlessly gesturing for me to follow.

We climbed into an unnatural silence.

My breath thundered out of my lungs.

My feet could not move fast enough.

As we neared a section of plateau where several small caves had formed in the cone, I shouted, "Children of forever, where are you? Where are you?"

Please brace yourself, Salmaya. Here is what unfolded next.

I saw a ghost. An apparition. For I would learn that it could not have been real.

Gela emerged from the mouth of one of the caves.

Gela alone!

She beckoned to us.

My heart flamed. My tongue went dead.

Then she retreated, and as we reached the cave, our children appeared to us, three in one as ever before. The sting of disappointment that they had not been separated was almost too much to bear.

But I fell at their feet and hugged and kissed them, and they returned those acts of affection—they were alive, and quite suddenly that was the only thing that mattered. Yet, in their embrace I felt a tension. A sorrow.

I looked into the eyes of Gela. Tears seized her face.

Seghers shoved roughly at my shoulder.

"Stay right here," he commanded.

I watched him swing up the cone another forty or fifty paces and then disappear around a shoulder of lava rock.

Good Face and Dune. The Gazelle Boy and his gazelle.

Our children sobbed.

And then I could not bear the tension any longer. I told our children not to follow as I scrambled in the direction Seghers had gone.

I found him hunkered down by what appeared to be the sleeping form of the Gazelle Boy. A gentle breeze played with the young man's long, black hair. Oddly, at first I felt no emotion whatsoever as Seghers pivoted away so that I could see a blossom of blood, a gunshot wound at the boy's heart.

And then what had been taken.

One of his ears. Several fingers. Many of his toes.

His sexual organs.

And both of his horns.

Beyond him lay his beautiful gazelle, mutilated. Gutted.

Nausea shook me like a rag. I vomited over and over.

And then I heard Seghers speak quietly, intensely as he lifted the boy as if he were merely injured. I could not believe what my companion said.

Tir. We must get him to Tir as quickly as possible. We must bring him back.

39

Dearest Salmaya, My Shelter From the Horrors,

In The Empty Too Much darkness can steal one's face. When that happens, one encounters a blankness beyond oneself.

Other dangers: the *mulitava*, an invisible gyre that rises like the undead from unnatural regions beneath the sand. The *mulitava* can trap one, causing one to walk endlessly in a circle like a ship foundered at sea.

I tell our children that you are close, Salmaya.

It helps them. It dries their tears.

40

Dearest Salmaya, Mother of Love Inexhaustible,

Grief draws reptiles and scorpions.

We must be watchful lest they nest in our hearts.

Our children seem to be recovering from the violence of the Hunters, but not from the Wasting. Without a new source of healing, how will they survive? I fear that as few as a dozen days remain for them.

Be near, Salmaya.

Send us a miracle.

41

Dearest Salmaya,

Seghers has disappeared within himself. His desire for revenge upon the Hunters threatens to erupt beyond control. He sharpens, unceasingly, the knife given him by Waralibi, The Listener at the Stone. I can smell his hunger for blood. I fear that he is losing his mind.

Without our children, I would lose mine. Let me tell you how they found strength within themselves. First, for several days after the murder of the Gazelle Boy, Gela and Simeo grew small horns resembling those sported by that wondrous young man. In turn, Forg bled sympathetically from a mysterious wound near his heart. Next, they took the one stone the Gazelle Boy created for them, and they passed it among themselves and chanted and sang until they were exhausted. The ritual, sad to say, finally shattered my nerves, causing me in a dark moment to shout angrily at them to stop.

We cannot continue like this.

42

Dearest Salmaya, Patient One,

You have waited, as I knew you would, and now, at last, I have the emotional distance that will allow me to recount what occurred when we took the body of the Gazelle Boy to Tir.

We set out desperately, on a desperate trail, for desperate purposes.

Seghers believed that in the living dark the dead could live again.

Hope filled my bloodstream.

Our children abided.

On a sweltering evening we entered The House of Dissection in Tir and a flock of witchy women descended upon the body of the Gazelle Boy. They knew what needed to be done; they began their revolting, yet salvific, work in earnest, digging deeply into the young man's body, pulling at innards as if they were preparing a holiday bird for roasting.

They believed, and Seghers apparently shared that belief, that an occult dissection could conquer death, that after a long night of mortality the hour of dawn would usher in an undying soul. The women tugged and cut and wrestled with the unresisting corpse until there transpired an amazing moment in which they gently raised the upper body of the Gazelle Boy so that he appeared to be sitting up, and as his head bobbed forward a black liquid gurgled from his mouth like vomit.

The women hissed.

Even the *smell* of the liquid was black, and in that blackness there seemed a chronicle of the history of shades of ebony.

Shielding our children from the sight, I looked on in absolute horror.

Then, from behind me, a scream that trumpeted.

A woman's scream.

It was Ngeza, the Gazelle Boy's mother.

She rushed forward demanding that the dissection cease. She reached for the body of her son. Her hands discovered the black liquid. For a small eternity, she gazed at her son's body and at the unknown spillage. In her eyes, it seemed to represent the sacred flow of his being. It was a mothering to her, and she to it. Reverently, she dabbed her fingers in its emergence and then, childlike, sucked on her fingertips.

At that sight, the witchy women wailed.

Seghers turned aside as if he had been blinded.

Moments later, Ngeza fell dead away.

Everyone knew that she was gone.

What more to tell?

Only this: as I gathered our children to leave, a hog-faced woman touched my arm with her cloven hoof and breathed these words to me: "Seek out The People of the Wild. Your only hope."

Seghers fled the scene. Our children and I followed.

I wanted only to never enter the village of Tir again.

Never, never, never, never, never.

43

Dearest Salmaya, May Your Spirit Stay Near,

With a new dawn, I find Seghers muttering about paths.

I go to him, and he stares at me, not seeing. He points west. More talk of paths. His inner compass is fixed upon The Black Mountains. He talks at me of not straying from the old paths, and I believe that at one distracted moment he whispered of The People of the Wild.

I crawl into his face, and I say, "What are you saying? What are you thinking? You must tell me what you are thinking?"

He shakes his head.

He appears to be staggering around in some inner realm, alone.

Then he winces as if in pain.

"The Hunters," he says. "There are forces in The Empty Too Much that one cannot allow to live. Things with no hint of human worth."

I shove at him and exclaim, "We can't undo the killings. Let go of it. We must push on."

He does not hear me.

He whispers Maeleeva's name. I sense that he is about to cry.

He rises and goes out away from our camp and stands with his back to me. He is listening. To his invisible gods? Are they dictating? Spouting poetry? Or are they speaking of a violence darker than midnight and too horrible for words? A necessary violence?

I do not know.

Before the sun rises higher than we can bear, we pack up

and head west. Always west. At the end of the day, our children are weak, having been punched unrelentingly by the indifferent heat.

In our tent we engage in the ritual of Mother Touch.

Your finger points us in the direction of hope.

We share tears.

Then I show them some of your wonderful drawings, those especially of insects: beetles, locusts, flies, ants. But particularly those of spiders—spiders with human faces.

"Your mother loves you very much," I say. "She would want you to have courage and not give up hope."

Gela and Simeo chortle, though they are weak. Forg quivers as if he is chilled to the bone.

Our children are dying.

Why can't I look the truth of that squarely in the eyes?

44

Dearest Salmaya, Let Not Your Vision Fade,

What rivers powerfully above our lives?

I long to return. I long to chase time back to the borders of my existence and away from the wordlessness of this wrong world—this place where the shapeless shape of darkness seeps into one's heart.

Sunset had the color of afterbirth, too sickly, too much blood—it was as if the day had been expelled, aborted. Now a ravenous darkness eats at me methodically like some giant insect nibbling upon a leaf.

"Seghers?"

I call out his name and realize suddenly that he is near, just beyond the fire, writing in his ancient book; writing, then listening in the direction of uncountable stars, then writing some more.

Are his gods demanding justice?

"Is it the Hunters?" I say to him, knowing in my gut that it is.

He closes his book and raises it gently to his forehead. He kisses the cover of it. He turns to me, and his eyes suck in the flames of our fire. I sense that he has decided something. I do not like the look of pity he offers to me. He speaks.

"There are things out there, hidden, breathing and not yet fully alive."

"What do you mean?"

He nods.

"Follow the old path. Do what you must do," he says.

An inexplicable hatred for him rises in my gorge. He walks away from the fire. He embraces Nightheart's neck and appears to whisper to him.

In our tent, Gela and Simeo converse with me in a consummate silence. Forg clings to my neck. Deep into the night, every true act of love between me and our children is wordless. I light a candle. I see or imagine that the skin of our children is turning different colors, the many shades of shadows. I think of certain desert lizards we have seen, those capable of becoming one with their background so that they may hide themselves.

Could it be that our children are hiding themselves from death?

I bury my nose in each of their small, frail bodies.

They smell of dying.

45

Salmaya, Always My Confessor,

I try not to conclude that we are in the wind and sand and heat of our final hours. This new morning our children refuse to eat or drink.

My mind spirals off into a dark galaxy of the past.

Salmaya, did I ever tell you that when I was a boy, my mother tried to kill herself? Yes, she did. She attempted to drown herself. She was rescued by a stranger. My father explained to me that she was sad, a sadness beyond disappointment, a sadness beyond alleviation. As children often do, I blamed myself for her sadness. I reckoned that I had not been a good child.

Why I think about this now, I do not know. Perhaps to take my mind off the terrible reality of our children.

Or perhaps this: when I woke, Seghers was gone.

He left Nightheart and Bloodfire and sufficient supplies for us.

Only the ghost of his madness lingers, silent and confused.

46

Dearest One, I Have Failed,

Salmaya, do you recall an old saying from The Land of Speaking Rivers, the one about the heart? Perhaps it is one you, in fact, told me. It runs like this: *The heart—for not to love is quite beyond its powers.*

I now know, more than ever before, the truth of that.

Several miserable days have passed.

I'm up at dawn feeding Nightheart and Bloodfire some seeds and thistle grass. I'm listening, as well, to a chorus of stillness. I look toward The Black Mountains, but a thick mist veils them. From that opaqueness beauty steps out despite the mysteries of dying that surround me and our children.

Mysteries of love, too.

And mysteries of violence.

Seghers has not returned.

Yesterday, Forg was bitten by a sand viper. There, I've said it.

Oh, Salmaya, things are going very badly for him. How could I have allowed it to happen? Inattentiveness at the least. Nights lately have seen the approach of many lizards and many scorpions. Crawly creatures on the move. Sand vipers, too.

One morning I entered the tent to find a scene of horrors: our children covered with large, emerald green scorpions. But a desert puzzle held sway, for even though it was a terrifying spectacle—that is, some of the scorpions rested upon their faces and across their eyes—not one of the many, many deadly stingers elected to strike. Why didn't they? It could have been that our children, gripped by their survival need to whisper their deeply personal prayers, soothed the scorpions, causing them to be non-aggressive. Or perhaps the rising sun warmed them enough to blunt their need to attack.

Who can say?

However, not more than an hour later, when I was spooning water into the mouth of Gela and Simeo, we heard Forg cry out and saw a horned venom carrier slither away and bury its cowardly self in the sand. Our son was bitten on the foot. It did not take long for an ugly swelling to begin. Now, today, the foot is purple, and I believe that the stummie between Simeo and Forg evidences paralysis. I have essentially no medications for snake bite.

In his hour of darkness, I must say that Forg is facing things bravely, stoically. Gela and Simeo pray and chant and touch at him lovingly. They give him the one stone to hold. They connect him to hope, and yet the poison in his veins has probably already begun to compromise their health as well.

We wait and watch.

I long for an unfolding of the merciful.

My darling, be near us in these our tortuous moments.

47

Praise Be To the Inexplicable Possibilities,

A full moon is waning, Salmaya. The Empty Too Much is canopied with stars. A cool breeze visits our camp from the south. I somehow keep expecting Seghers to return. Nightheart is lying down. Bloodfire would, but the cut on his underbelly is too painful, I believe.

And so, my dearest one, this is what occurred.

With only moonlight slicing in to illuminate the scene in our tent, we tendered our love to Forg. I pressed a cold rag onto his burning forehead; Gela and Simeo concentrated their healing energies as intensely as possible. But they, themselves, were suffering the effects of the viper's poison.

I held my breath in a feckless gesture of defiance.

I was losing our children. I could not prevent the inevitable.

Nearly oblivious to everything else, I thought suddenly that I heard Nightheart whinny, a sound of warning that an intruder approached. I stiffened. The soft paws of some animal neared the tent. I pressed our children to me in a many angled round of protection.

I heard panting.

"Get away!" I shouted.

The thing at the entrance to the tent pulled back, then a face—the face of a cheetah ghosted into view. As I started to shout again, the visage of the large cat shifted.

And the eagerly meaningful expression of Tovelmi took its place.

The Girl With Eyes of the Wind.

Her nose jittered. She frowned.

"I can help," she said. "But it's got to be quick."

"Come in, please," I said. "It's a viper bite."

She knew that, of course. I lighted a candle and got out of the way as she swung around and examined the bite area. Then, like a cat lapping at a bowl of milk, she stroked the wound with her tongue. I believe she flashed an understanding smile at Forg before nudging him with the side of her head. She may even have purred slightly, deep in her throat.

"We need to use your camel," she said to me, her eyes dilated and insistent.

"He's a poor old, mostly worthless beast," I said.

"We need what's in his guts," she said.

After I carried our children out to Bloodfire, Tovelmi slipped something into Bloodfire's mouth so that he would stand still and put up with what came next. A glint of a knife blade and a very precise slit into the animal's belly. Some blood pulsed out as well as some yellowish liquid.

"Get the child's foot in there," she exclaimed.

I hesitated. She hissed something I didn't understand, and it spurred me. Forg's foot slid into the opening just like into a sandal. Bloodfire squawked a bit. Stomped one hoof. Tovelmi held our son's foot inside. Bloodfire belched twice and bellowed once.

A minute or so later that part of the process was over.

I took our children back to the tent while Tovelmi heated some mixture known only to her and the gods. She stirred a small pot over a fire she ignited more quickly than seemed possible. The concoction aboil, she cooled it with water and her own spit, and together we forced open Forg's lips and made him drink most of the thick substance. What remained of it Tovelmi rubbed directly on to the bite area. From a tiny bottle she gave Gela and Simeo a drink or two of some black liquid to combat what the venom was doing to them.

Almost magically, in no more than ten minutes, our children were peacefully asleep. Tovelmi and I built up a new fire, and I stared into her remarkable eyes and choked out a thank you. I trembled with awe and appreciation. She glanced away as if she suddenly regretted something.

"Will you stay with us?" I said.

She shook her head.

"You don't understand my life," she said.

And I just let all my concerns flow out: the fact that Seghers had vanished, the need to get to The Black Mountains and to find The People of the Wild, and my deep fears that even though the snake bite crisis might be over, the Wasting continued to threaten our children.

"They're dying," I pleaded.

She nodded.

"You're headed the right way," she said. "I can't be with you." Those incredible eyes teared up, and when she spoke again, it was in a whisper: "I can't be with you."

I felt cold and hollow.

She gave me directions on what to do for our children in the morning. I reached for her. I think I just wanted to touch her. Thank her in some way beyond my understanding, beyond the failure of language.

But she jolted back. She nervously brushed her long hair away from her face and whispered something more, a few words that I couldn't hear. She began to walk towards the darkness, ignoring my calls after her, and when she made it to the edge of the firelight expanse, she dropped to all fours and soon the young woman of her gave way to the cheetah-self within.

Moonlight spotted her for several seconds.

Then the night claimed her as she ran faster than any wind, faster even than my beating heart.

48

Dearest Salmaya,

Please understand.

This shall be my last letter to you. The episode with Forg's near death stormed through me with a bitterly cold wind of reality. I must face my self-delusions.

I have lied to myself about your spirit being near.

But it was a necessary lie. It kept me sane. Writing these letters to your imaginary presence helped me immensely. I must now, however, let the phantasm of you go. Your ghost never actually arrived. You are not, I believe, off in the distant beyond in some heavenly realm waiting for me and our children to join you. No, you have returned to the same great darkness and deep peace from which you came—from which we all came and to which, one day, we shall all arrive.

The memory of your astonishing love will always be with us.

I sense that you would want two things regarding the future: first, that I continue to pursue the healing of our children and to ensure, if possible, meaningful lives for them; second, I believe that you would want me to find another love, another womanly companion in order to be complete and whole. Our children fill my life, and yet I am lonely.

So very lonely.

In the shattering weakness that I feel, I want to ask for your forgiveness, but I know that you would dismiss such a gesture. Seghers once told me that courage is much more necessary than hope. I sense at this moment that he was right.

I must continue writing of this quest into The Empty Too Much.

Now, though, my letters will be addressed to myself, or, rather to the *Other I Am*, a more authentic self, one that will serve as my confessor.

As I write this, I am mostly sane, yet I am being pursued by fears.

I have learned a profound lesson: memory is salvation, but to live life more livingly one must enter fully into the unprotected present.

49

To the Other I Am,

I feel bloodless. The Empty Too Much has vampired me.

My children are my world and the only reason for existing.

Nearly a week has now passed since Forg's recovery. Tovelmi's prescription for his return to health has worked for the most part, and Gela and Simeo are cheered by his escape from death. The awful reality, however, is that the Wasting continues to inhabit all three of them, insistent, implacable— desiring to test the limits of their mortality.

And this: we are dangerously low on water.

I need Seghers.

In a different way, I need Tovelmi, for she is, I realize, alive in my thoughts and perhaps in my heart.

While I can't be certain, I believe that we have not strayed much from the old path to The Black Mountains. At times we track across a surreal landscape of fissures, faults and several boiling lakes of lava. We keep our distance from the intense heat of those lakes. Sometimes a weird beauty emerges where sulfur and algae wed to generate hot springs and pools of water green as an unripe lemon. We sight salt caravans and camel traders on the southern horizon. Sometimes our track narrows and we pass near ramparts of salt, mud and soft rock looming in tortuous shapes sculpted by the wind.

I watch for leopards. And I am aware that we are constantly negotiating the border between the known and the unknown and that we are held in the grip of a dark time zone in which creatures rarely seen emerge from the shadows.

Seghers once spoke of this mysterious time as *the blue hour.*
A portal to another world? Yes, perhaps.

Everything that rises before my eyes is sinister, predatory.
We cross dry beds of seasonal rivers, enter copses of
gnarled, ancient fig trees. I grow helplessly terrified of
leopards. They are among the rocks. Nightheart hears them,
smells them, tastes them. Strange and bizarre owls make
their presence known—their hoots range from eerie sighs to
warning growls.

Another dawn.

My children are thirsty; Nightheart and Bloodfire are
thirsty; The desert light is hallucinatory. I look out and deny
to myself that I see a lone traveler. Only a mirage. A figment.
But the temptation is too much.

"Do you have water?" I call out.

My words echo in the teeth of the wind and the heat.

The traveler stops.

My chest burns with hope.

"Please. Do you have water? My children. For my children."

He is an old man in filthy rags. He is carrying a bundle.
Could it be a water cask?

Twenty paces from me, he stops, and I stagger to him,
muttering, "Water, please water. Please."

He holds out the bundle for me to view, and I am startled.
It is a small child. No, not precisely a child. When the traveler
pulls back the dusty corner of a blanket, I see the face—half
human, half ape. I pitch back from it. The traveler shakes his
head.

"I have no water," he says.

When my disappointment finally wanes, I say, "Where are
you going?"

His response almost knocks my legs out from under me.

"To The Black Mountains. To The People of the Wild." Then
he gestures with his chin towards the ape child. "For him."

And I understand.

He tells me that there is water up ahead, a small lake of
mostly fresh water. *"Furzi ama"* he calls it.

"What do those words mean?" I say.

He blinks into the wind. Then he mutters, "Waters of Despair."

Without further ado, he moves on. I want, of course, to ask him if we can join him. There is, however, something in the utter desolation of him that silences my tongue.

He could not, I believe, abide company.

50

To the Other I Am,

The lake—*Furzi ama*—was shrouded in fog, great patches of it blocking the sun and smothering the surface of the water. Exhausted when we finally reached its shore, I hurried about preparing a camp, building a fire and mashing dates into a paste, hoping my children would have an appetite. I filled a water cask with what the lake had to offer: a mossy, slightly acrid tasting liquid.

To me, not the *Waters of Despair*, but rather the waters of survival.

Nightheart and Bloodfire drank until they stumbled under the refreshing weight of quenching their thirsts.

By late morning the fog burned away.

Sunlight, in vicious spears, angled down hotly and spawned an eye-blistering glare. I stayed in the tent with my children, and I thought about final things. Food and water seemed not to revive my dear ones. They were sluggish and feverish. They could not control their bodily functions—our tent smelled of urine despite my efforts to keep them cleaned up. Gela cried. To my surprise, Simeo did not attempt to console her. It was a bad sign.

I hunkered down in front of Forg and asked how he was doing.

He said nothing at first. He merely patted upon the useless stummie.

"It's dead, isn't it?" he said.

I nodded.

"The viper's poison was too strong," I added.

Then he looked at me with something like wonder in his eyes.

"It was so beautiful," he murmured. "The viper. It bit me and crawled away, and it was so beautiful. Like gold and diamonds."

Words choked in my throat.

"Yes," was all I could manage.

By twilight the three of them had worsened.

Gela and Simeo began to chant. It sounded like a dirge. I wanted to ask them to stop, but I couldn't. Forg held the one stone and raised it to his lips and kissed it. I didn't know what his gesture meant.

But I knew that my children were dying.

I pushed myself out of the tent and went to where Nightheart was standing, and I hugged his neck and I sobbed. My chest was wracked with sadness. I heaved, and my tears wetted that marvelous animal's neck. Then I gradually got a hold of myself. I built a new fire. I checked on Bloodfire's wound.

I sat and drank in the lovely surface of the lake.

I thought of Salmaya.

I wouldn't ask her again to forgive me; I would, however, make an effort to forgive myself whether I deserved it or not.

I thought of Tovelmi.

No, I didn't know or understand her life.

I understood nothing about The Empty Too Much.

My children were dying.

What else was there to know?

How long did I sit staring at those waters?

As long as my self-pity had me in its grasp.

With the fall of a deeper darkness around me, I began to hear a macabre chuckling. Not hyenas. Not night birds. Point by point then pairs of red dots floated on the surface of the lake. Something glided. Something watched. Something was watching me.

Crocodiles.

I shuddered.

When I went back inside the tent, I hugged each one of my children. I told them separately how much love I felt for him or her.

"Sleep well," I told them. "In the morning, we'll go out into the lake. We'll play in it. Enjoy ourselves. Get good and clean."

I smiled.

Gela and Simeo were silent.

It was Forg who spoke.

"Father," he said, "we know. We know."

I was trembling. My voice was shaky.

"It's best for all of us," I said. "All of us. I just don't know what else to do."

I started to add: Forgive me. Instead, I leaned into them, and I felt the soothing, unbelievably loving and gentle touching of their tiny fingers.

51

To the Other I Am,

I blamed Seghers for everything, including for the spiral down of the health of my children. He abandoned us. Our guide. His maniacal need for revenge against the Hunters spun him off into the Neverwhere of madness—if he had stayed and acted responsibly we might have already reached The Black Mountains and The People of the Wild.

Instead.

May the gods themselves damn you, damn you, Seghers!

So. Well, thus it is.

No fog or mist this morning. Sun bright, ironically beautiful. But we have come to the end—my children and I. They have suffered long enough. *We* have suffered long enough. I failed in my quest to find healing for them.

I sit here upon the shore of this lovely, indifferent lake, and I think about the word *tragedy*: this is *not* a tragedy with all its attendant grandeur but rather the smaller sadness of a private defeat.

An act of courage? Would that it were. But I think that courage truly does not earn redemption; those, however, who locate courage deep within deserve to declare themselves to be something higher than animals.

If the gods asked me to choose between knowing everything or knowing nothing, I would simply walk away. Or, better yet, I would summon up the resolve to say that I choose to know goodness.

The laughing response of those same gods would not crush me.

Well, enough of this idle confession to my other self.

52

To the Long Suffering Other I Am,

The crocodiles seem wary of the splashing. At least, it appears that they are giving us a wide berth, floating—like rough-barked logs—away from us or no closer than parallel. Some remain on the shore, basking in the eager sun, warming up the ancient coldness of their blood. Or maybe they're simply not hungry this morning, not for human flesh that is.

As my children churn the water and giggle, I glance around at the tangled, sun-speared lake. I say tangled, for ropes of green kelp and stringy roots of hyacinth drift on or just below the surface. Parts of the shore are lined with spiky willows and cane. Birds are chirping and diving after insects. There is virtually no wind. There is an abundance of quiet beauty.

But I will not change my mind.

"*Father! Father! Father!*" Gela chortles. Simeo has water in his eyes and rubs at the sting.

As I hold them, buoyant in their diminished weight, I find that Forg is staring at me; in his expression I read, *Go ahead and get this over with.*

Why am I hesitating? This is for the best.

I tug them out into what I assume is deeper water. I'm guessing that the bottom is fifteen to twenty feet. Plenty deep enough. And I struggle with a need to say something more—words of farewell, a final expression of love. My mind, however, is sludgy. I am as listless and lazy as the crocs.

Suddenly all three children are beating the water and laughing, enjoying themselves, and I can't prevent a smile from seizing my face. They issue tiny, high-pitched screams of joy. I scream with them, more of a nervous run of shouts, I suppose.

And the question: *How to do this?*

I had vaguely imagined diving below their feet and gently, though firmly, pulling them under, down, down, down, and not letting go until the final letting go took over naturally.

All four of us. To a watery grave.

So we splash and empty our lungs and exhaust our vocal chords.

I strangle a sob.

I have a fleeting thought of Salmaya.

And, once again, Forg is staring at me. He is shaming me. I look away. Then I feel his fingertips tapping my shoulder.

In his hand is the one rock, the rock that they have shared since the Gazelle Boy took their three smaller rocks and created this one and only one. His voice low, he says to me, "Tell us to dive after the rock. Like a game. A game."

It's something close to a brilliant suggestion. Yes, I can imagine it playing out.

An end game. Our deaths together. The deaths within us. A game.

Almost fun.

I take the rock from Forg.

I get the attention of my three children.

I explain the game: we'll let the rock sink and then we'll all go to the bottom after it. Like diving for pearls. Together. A game.

But I don't, of course, say that it's a game we cannot win.

53

To the Witness of Who I Am,

The hand that grasped me was very small. Yet strong. An almost supernatural strength.

Being dragged to the surface, I recall now coughing out a mouthful of water and looking about wildly for my children; I did not see them, nor did I see our rescuer until I was twenty or thirty feet above the water. Yes, *above.*

Out of my body.

Like a leaping fish or a gliding bird. Or, perhaps, a hovering angel.

Then a snap and crackle when I slammed back into my chest as I splashed and a thin arm pulled at me, yoking my armpit. I gasped and coughed some more. And I knew only that somehow I was alive. Alive in the blissful presence of the sun and all the other elements.

It took ages, it seemed, for me to speak, and when I did, I yelled at the top of my lungs: "My children! My children!"

And the response of the softest, sleepiest voice I had ever heard: "They are saved. They are saved," it said.

Time passing, passing, passing.

Late afternoon, twilight nearing, I assumed, because of the westward slant of the defeated sun. A good blaze of a fire and the best sound I could imagine: the murmurings of my children. I pushed up out of my stupor, and there, on her knees staring at me—into me—was an unaccountably surrealistic-looking woman whose face transcended age somehow and whose eyes, though penetrating, were barely open, barely alive, it seemed.

"I am *Thyrza nht Ulli*," she said, a voice totally lacking in energy and nearly sexless.

But I could only call her by what immediately came to me: The Hungry Girl.

When she stood up, so did I.

How to describe her?

Thin. As thin as a person might possibly be. I seemed to be seeing a person who had never eaten. Even her hands were starving. Her skin was bronzed, and she wore a long, bronze-colored skirt with no shoes. Her hair, also bronze, fell in two braids just past her shoulders. Smooth and skeletal, her face seemed incapable of a smile or any other emotive expression, for that matter. Her lips appeared to be permanently closed—could she speak without parting them? I looked at her a moment, taking in the whole of her, and then I instantly glanced away: she was naked from the waist up, but she had no breasts except for a slight swell around each nipple. Her ribs were prominent.

I flushed from a candle of embarrassment within.

When I looked back at her, I could see that her eyes remained closed.

The Hungry Girl. Our savior.

And I found that I was too tired or too much in shock to speak. I went to my children and hugged them and they showered me with fingertips.

Thus began a string of days in which The Hungry Girl tended to us. She did so even as she continued on her trek to the place where she would lie down near the blood of the earth and the wounds of the stones and die the only death she had ever been promised.

54

To the Other I Am Becoming,

In the days of The Hungry Girl, I often found myself remembering snatches of poetry, probably from poems Salmaya had read to me. One quatrain rambled back from the echoes of the past and made me smile. It went like this:

And the harlot walks alone
like a rumor through the street,
her buttocks bright as surging lamps,
her smile as old as stone.

As I lazed around both useless and helpless, The Hungry Girl gathered shoots of a sugary cane and spiky reeds as well as gobs of dark green kelp from the lake. She mashed and mixed the ingredients into a dish that resembled spinach. And this she fed to my children over and above my protests and questions. She seemed to know what she was doing.

But I must admit that the first night after that green dosage, my children waned, grew much worse. I exclaimed my displeasure to The Hungry Girl. She barely acknowledged my concerns. By mid-morning, my children revived. They sang. They chanted. They drew The Hungry Girl into their love and their appreciation. Was she pleased? I saw no evidence of it.

That evening we talked, she and I, as we sat by the fire.

"Are they healed? I said. Has the Wasting run its course?" Almost imperceptibly she shook her head.

So I pressed her: "What now? How much longer do they have?"

"Another moon," she said.

More words flowed from her, as in a toneless, fleshless, corpse-like voice she explained that she lacked the power to make them completely well. Only The People of the Wild possessed that facility.

My anxiety raged in me.

"What will The People of the Wild do for them?" I demanded. "How is it possible to heal them?"

She stared at me as if she doubted I could understand. I almost wanted to strike her. Her eyelids opened more so than ever before and she said, "They will give them an appetite for life. They will give them a place of their own. A home."

"But they have a home," I countered. "With me. Their father."

She lapsed into a stillness that was astonishing. Then she rose and walked out into the shadows.

After I had said good night to my children, I saw to Nightheart and Bloodfire, and I longed to talk with Seghers. Where was that vengeful, crazed bastard? I needed him to explain what was happening. Positioning myself close to the flames, I could not see where The Hungry Girl had gone—perhaps she, too, had abandoned us. I truly had no idea. I sat and rocked back and forth, entertaining fleeting images of childhood, of the home I once had. When those images dissolved, I began to sense voices—*buried voices*—not out in the gathering darkness but rather *beneath* the campsite.

Voices I could *feel* yet not *hear*.

I believe they spoke of absence.

I sat until the after midnight breezes arrived, and quite suddenly I heard the four great vowels of the wind pouring out of the hidden throat of the sky.

55

To the Other I Have Never Been,

We moved West Northwest.

We left behind the Waters of Despair.

We left behind the one and only one stone.

By day, my children thrived, even during sandstorms and broiling heat. They adored The Hungry Girl, and it seemed that to show her their appreciation they developed wild talents and performed extraordinary little acts of magic.

Gela, for example, would work up a mouthful of spittle, close her eyes tightly and then round her lips open as if to blow a bubble. What emerged from her, from some unknown, creative cells of her being, were totally unique butterfly-like creatures the color of clear glass; they hovered by her nose before winging out into the Everywhere.

For his part, Simeo, always the spiritually minded, commanded the attention of The Hungry Girl through a stunning exercise of concentration through which he could—with no wind stirring—cause sand and dust to swirl and swirl and then to shape the particles into angelic figures rising and, seemingly, offering their blessings before tearing themselves apart and falling back into the elements from which they came.

I was amazed.

Then Forg. Even Forg.

In his moment, he would select small rocks of various shapes and colors, squeeze them in the palm of his hand and magically turn them into quite beautiful, jewel-like forms. But his performance did not stop there. He would line the jewels at his feet, then with a twirl and a twist of his fingers, each jewel would morph into a viper, a colorfully lovely, tiny viper. At the clap of his hands, each serpent would slither away never to be seen again.

The Hungry Girl smiled ever so slightly at these displays, but I sensed that they did not, in the least, surprise her. To her, it seemed that everything could be expected.

The following day we received a visitor.

56

To the Witness of These Mysteries,

She called herself the lover of *Thyrza nht Ulli*.

Because the two of them fell into an affectionate embrace, I had no reason to doubt her claim. She spoke again, and her words blossomed as a name: *Zueenoto pvitacra gdeur*. I pieced together enough of it to know that some combination of *feet* and *death* was indicated. Our visitor smiled, her teeth magnificently white against her chocolate skin.

"It means *Her Feet Took Hold on Death*," she said.

I returned her smile, yet mine was cautious, timid.

"The women of The Empty Too Much have fascinating names," I returned.

Her pretty and wide-set eyes swung up to the sky and off to the nearest rock formations and the hard scrabble of sand and dust and thirsty plants. She chuckled softly, then quickly frowned.

"The Empty Too Much," she murmured, shaking her head— "everything good dies here."

Somewhere I had heard those words before. Or had I only imagined them?

"But *not* my children," I exclaimed. "Now I know more than ever before that I can't let them die." I paused. My imperative tone sounded foolish to me. No other remark came to mind.

Holding the hand of The Hungry Girl, our visitor reached her other hand inside her white robe and pulled forth the smallest deer I have ever seen—no larger than a kitten.

"The secret of all hearts remains beyond our daylight vision," she said, smiling down first at the deer and then at The Hungry Girl before embracing my face with her eyes and adding, "This is *Messenger,* and *she* is my child, but one day The Empty Too Much will welcome her to the forever darkness."

A fleeting thought of what she meant by *my child* passed through my thoughts, but instead of addressing it, I studied her some more: the purple turban on her head, the flawless skin oddly marked with three circles the size of a large coins, one on each cheek and one on her forehead. Each circle had a yellow dot at its center.

Night again brought conversation. While The Hungry Girl and our visitor's tiny deer spent time with my children, I longed to talk with Zueenoto, and she seemed willing and receptive. We began with The Hungry Girl's rescue of me and my children.

"She could not allow your destruction," Zueenoto explained. "She is incapable of passing up or ignoring an opportunity to save someone. It's in her blood. But she is nearing her end."

"What do you mean?"

"She's going where others like her go to die."

"These others are very thin, too?"

"Yes. It's a secret group. A mystery tribe or cult. I'm not one of them. In fact,

Thyrza was exiled because of our love—woman to woman love, you see."

I found myself wanting to know much more about The Hungry Girl, for she was extraordinarily strange. Zueenoto appeared happy to talk about her lover.

"Thyrza is closer to the dead than to the living. You must try to understand that, for her and others like her, hunger is a sacred state of the body. She exists in a state of hunger possession. It allows her to connect with the desert wisdom of the living dead."

"Why must she die?" I asked.

"Because her death calls. It … *commands.* She must obey."

We began then to talk about The Empty Too Much, and I was surprised to learn that she knew or was aware of virtually everyone I had encountered: Seghers and Maeleeva, the Witch

Diggers, the Sisters of the Barren, the Breath Charmer, Waralibi, the Gazelle Boy, the inhabitants of the village of Tir. She even had a passing friendship with Tovelmi—lovely, lovely Tovelmi.

"And The People of the Wild—what about them?" I said.

"They are spirit beings. One can know only a little about such entities."

"Can they heal my children?"

A smile rippled across her amazing face.

Her eyes twinkled.

"They can heal the universe."

57

To the Other I Am,

Dawn. The chosen hour of good, but also the bewitching time among all others in the desert. I was learning that The Empty Too Much offers two great visions: *enchantment* and *death*. Zueenoto had given me even more understanding of this alien realm, speaking of its inhabitants as dreamers, restless souls, lovers of the chimera but also vicious ones—like the Hunters—wedded to a white veil of violence. She reaffirmed for me that hope leads to the grave. Always, though, she alluded to The Empty Too Much as a sublimely fantastic country, a place that at times reveals its soul to one.

I believed that Seghers would agree.

As I stirred and moved about to prepare myself and my children for another day, I noticed that The Hungry Girl had risen from a lover's embrace with Zueenoto and had wandered off to face the rising sun.

And then.

She sat down as if to plant herself in the sand; she raised her hands above her head, lowered them, and chanted something indistinct. What followed challenged my sense of reality: two copies—exact copies—of herself materialized, the two other figures of her joining her at her spine.

A three-in-one.

Like my children.

When she returned to camp, she had molted the other two figures. She sat down beside me as if nothing had happened.

I cleared my throat.

"I saw," I said. "I saw what occurred … out there."

She turned to face me. Almost smiled. Deflected my embarrassment.

"Yes. I was like your children once."

"And you were healed? Separated, I mean—is that it?"

"Being three-in-one is a blessing," she murmured.

"Why? How so?"

She paused for an uncomfortable passing of seconds.

"Because it causes you to become close to wholeness. Three-in-one, always in search of the fourth. Four is the number of completeness—the four winds, the four seasons."

"So then, why? That is …why are you *you*? Why just *one* of you?"

Her expression appeared to sink into a memory that was not salvation.

"I was not allowed to choose," she said.

And with that she moved to awaken Zueenoto.

Later we journeyed on through the heat and the indifferent if not unfriendly landscape. Beyond ourselves and our animals, our companions were wind and sand and dust and lifeless scatterings of rocks and dying plants. Towards evening and still another campsite, the habitual chorus of hyena, owls, wild dogs and, a new member, leopards with their throaty coughs.

My children taught me through their love to be almost human again. "Forgive me," I told them numerous times, for what I intended. Gela and Simeo always responded by kissing my face. Forg would shake his head, a gesture I simply could not read.

58

To the Beauty of Mystery and the Mystery of Beauty,

Like skeletons in a noose, we hang from this brilliant morning. Yet, much too soon, the jaws of the wind-driven sand threaten to consume us when invisible powers cut us down and we run to safety.

There is also a sense this morning that the gods themselves are confused, or as if they're waiting for *holy words* to come walking across the desert to greet and worship them.

Where do the gods live?

Seghers claimed once that it was at the bottom of oblivion, a lightless pit, among serpents.

I think of Salmaya. Wouldn't she remind me to open my eyes to the mystic beauty of the moon and to accept the old thirst in my bones? Stay on the quest. Wait for what wants to come.

I am weary.

We are taking a vital detour slightly to the north. To where The Hungry Girl must go. Once she reaches there, my children and I will, along with Nightheart and Bloodfire, turn directly west to The Black Mountains.

To The People of the Wild.

And as to the fate then of Zueenoto and Messenger? I do not know.

Early afternoon, we came to a village—Methruska—where we stop for water and what meager foodstuffs might be available. I keep my children out of sight. It is an ancient village, more ancient than most, for it has many towers, rock towers, twenty to thirty feet in height and rather obelisk in shape, but most are crumbling and decaying as if some terrible plague has overtaken them. The Hungry Girl explains that the towers were built mainly for protective shelter during wars with roaming bands of lawless warriors; there were blood feuds of unknown origin.

But now the towers are used to store hay and grain, for to the east of the village lie fertile fields, green patches watered from springs. We see pens of hogs and small herds of goats, some of which stroll with impunity through the streets. We see few people. One is a lone woman who when she saw us, scrambled out of sight, her steps quick and fearful. In the void left behind, The Hungry Girl whispered to me that dead villagers were buried under the sandy, rocky streets in unmarked graves. Just west of the village, we saw the pasturing of a breed of large cattle with bison features. Beyond that point, I glanced back over my shoulder at those lonely, forbidding towers, and I experienced a chill.

That night The Hungry Girl invited us to share a last supper.

Over a roaring fire, Zueenoto prepared a flatbread flecked with herbs and rounded into a mandala. We tore off pieces of it, and we ate in silence and reverence. When we had finished the meal, The Hungry Girl thanked us.

And in her own inimical way, she blessed us.

59

To Being Alone with the Alone,

By late morning of the following day we had climbed to the rim of a small, volcanic caldera, its black walls as shiny as coal and loaded with memories of violence and fire. The scene that spread out down below nearly a hundred feet was eerily breathtaking: sprawling piles of bones as white as the moon, the remnants of the brothers and sisters of The Hungry Girl.

Stoically she stood with us on the knife blade edge of the caldera, wind whipping her bronzed face; she said goodbye to my children, embracing them, whispering mystical things to them that, no doubt, they and only they understood. Then she touched my shoulder and, under her breath, she said, "Prepare yourself for difficulties you cannot imagine. I wish you well. I wish you the capacity to know *otherness*, to accept it, to live it."

Dizzied by her words, I nodded.

I thought momentarily of Maeleeva.

The Hungry Girl turned to the waiting figures of Zueenoto and Messenger. Love suddenly surrounded the three of them like a rose red mist. The two women kissed like lovers, and like lovers they parted as ones who would be together somewhere again forever, even if only in the darkness.

The Hungry Girl made her way down, down, down, climbing, climbing, climbing into her death. She went, it seemed to me, as if acting a theatrical part, and found her spot on her final stage where the final curtain would close. She curled up against the impossible shine of black rock, her face turned away from us, and before we had even begun to depart, we knew somehow that she had passed, her hunger for dying met. And she was filled with the food of a strangely nourishing mortality.

That evening I said to Zueenoto: "Will you continue with us? You are welcome to."

"No. I must find whoever, whatever now seeks me."

"How can you know which way to go?"

She smiled and petted the precious head of her tiny deer.

"You forget, she said. I have Messenger."

So she stayed the night at our camp.

In the morning, as I expected, only an apparition of her beautiful face remained with us.

"My children," I said, "we are going West. The People of the Wild await us."

60

To the Other Who Knows the Way,

I learned the true color of darkness.
This is how it happened.
This is how it began.
With a mirror. My children grew obsessed with a need to see each other. The only means to accomplish this was through a hand mirror that I had brought along. It was one used years ago by Salmaya. When alone I sometimes glanced into it hoping that it had, impossibly, trapped the image/reflection of her beautiful face on its surface. Alas, no. But I would position it out away from Gela so that she could see Simeo, and he her. They would smile and giggle and wink at each other, no end to their delight. Then I would do a similar positioning of the mirror for Simeo and Forg and then finally for Forg and Gela. They marveled, I believed, both in how similar they appeared, and yet also how different. That they were, in fact, distinct and separate human creatures. My response was always a stab of sadness as I continued to imagine that only *one* of them might survive the eventual healing and necessary separation somewhere in the future. Which one? I could never decide. No, the truth is that I wouldn't allow myself to decide.

We were in our tent on a warm, breezy afternoon when things changed.

Over their soft laughter and chortling as they shared and embraced the mirror images of each other, I heard a distant howl. It alarmed me.

"Stay here," I told them.

I crawled out of the tent and saw Hell devouring the horizon. In the baking heat, my body suddenly went cold.

It was too late to pull up stakes and seek the shelter of rocks a quarter of a mile away. My mind shifted into the most simplistic linear mode possible: I thought of what Seghers would do. I ran out to where I had tethered Nightheart and Bloodfire. I untied them and slapped each on the rump and shouted for each to go. "Run. Save yourself." Nightheart, connected intuitively as he was to what approached, obeyed immediately. Bloodfire, obtuse as well as stubborn, took more coaxing and harder slaps on the rump before he trotted off in the direction Nightheart had gone.

I raced back to our tent, turned once to face the nearing howl, and I gasped.

The color of darkness as it attacked had three levels: the first and lowest was a blue-blackness shimmering out of a magnificent spiral of thousands and thousands of black flies, their buzzing hellish and insistent; the second level was a burning, coppery color shining out from a moving curtain of locusts, their wings clicking like the chattering of the teeth of a monster; and the third and highest level of color was a milky brown looming mushroom cloud of dust that generated evil, licking tongues of lightning.

We are doomed, I thought to myself.

We were to be added to the long, ancient list of desert martyrs.

"Father! Father! Father!"

The fear in their small voices slammed into me inside the tent. I covered them in our black cape of cloth and burrowed under with them; they trembled hotly and tearfully, and I told them to be still and to think of their wonderful mother who was, at that horrible moment, somehow with them. Protecting them. I almost believed it myself.

The growl of the black flies and the locusts and the dust roller reached a deafening level. Our tent whipped and snapped and popped in the gale. The black flies reached us first, stabbing, stinging at the cape that covered us. Their buzz blotted out every other possible sound. I hugged at my children; their whimpers cut into my heart.

And then, when after a nightmare of minutes, I began to feel that we might weather the assault, I reached for Gela, my fingers accidentally pressing between her lips, I found that her mouth was wet and sticky and full.

Filled with black flies!

Instinctively, I yanked off the cape and swung it to beat off the winged invaders. It seemed to do little good. Each of us soon was choking on the gouts of flies as they entered our ears and noses and spread open our lips as if grotesquely desiring to give us sustenance.

The locusts, surprisingly, offered us a respite.

With their mad, dead wild clicking, they chased off the black flies as they swarmed into our tent, collapsing it and thus, ironically, minimizing the effect of their stampeding force. But the sound of them, the *feel* of them was utterly horrific. They bit at us and tore at us, eating at our clothing and at our skin. There was no way and nothing to stop them until the third wave fisted into us.

The massive dust cloud walking on strokes of lightning.

We would not only die, but we would also be buried by the avalanche of screaming, raging dust.

We waited.

We braced ourselves for the worst.

Flashes of lightning pulsed behind my closed eyes.

"I love you," I said again and again to my children.

"Father, Father, Father."

Then I called out to the gods.

At the top of my voice, I called.

The wind thundered closer, closer, closer.

A river of dust began to stream over the top of us.

A flood of horror.

But then.

The incessant roar lifted even as it began to sweep us away.

Seconds passed.

I listened.

And we were baptized in silence.

The darkness suddenly, inexplicably lifted.

I pushed the tent from us and struggled to my feet.

And what I saw was too amazing for words.

61

To the One Who Listens Always,

The approach of Nightheart and a four-legged shadow.

I blinked my eyes and looked over my shoulder to the east: the plague of flies and locusts and the dust cloud apocalypse had dissipated. Something miraculous had occurred, and I could not understand it except to assume that the presence of Nightheart and his strange companion had somehow chased the threat away.

As I gathered my children and pointed them in the direction of our saviors, they cheered and clapped and sang and whistled. I greeted Nightheart and hugged his neck; he neighed softly, and then he stepped aside as if presenting someone of royal stature.

It was a black colt. A foal. A very small, not quite yearling colt, emaciated, stumbling, but when he fixed one of his dark, dark eyes upon me I was galvanized. An instant bond formed between us—I have no idea why. When I neared him, he shied slightly before holding his ground to allow me to look him over.

He was extraordinary.

A zebra colt.

What's so amazing about that?

He was pure black. Nary a hint of white.

Every inch of him black, I say—a rarity among all rarities.

A freak of nature. A beautiful, little piece of monstrosity.

I stroked one of his ears.

"Thank you," I whispered. "Thank you for your presence."

I really didn't know what I meant.

Nightheart nosed his way over, and I embraced both beasts. "Thank you for chasing off all of those demons."

So moved was I that I chuckled to myself through the threat of tears and shook my head. I helped my children get close enough to say hello to our remarkable, new visitor. They, too, felt the birth of an immediate relationship with the stunning colt; they, too, deeply appreciated his arrival.

Even Bloodfire, who had made his way back to our camp, trundled over to see our visitor and sniff at him in camel wonder. Then once again I turned to Nightheart and hugged and petted his neck.

"You, sir," I said, "did this, didn't you? You found this marvelous creature and brought him to us. You knew he had power over those demons."

And so in the next couple of days we tended to the zebra colt. We fed him grain, and we gathered what desert grasses we could find; we saw to it that he had water. There was, however, no mother's milk for him, and that worried me. When my children asked where the colt came from, I had to speculate: perhaps his mother had been killed by a leopard or a black-maned, desert lion—or perhaps because of his most unusual coloration, he had been shunned by the herd to which he belonged. Perhaps he had been exiled and Nightheart had led him to us—to save him and us and to join our family.

"Father, Father, Father, what is his name?" my children chorused.

"I don't know," I said.

And so they occupied themselves with naming until something occurred to me. At which point I hunkered down to them and said, "I have it. Let's call him *Darkling*."

And so we did.

The very next dawn I went to the colt with a handful of parched grass. As he nibbled it from my fingers, I said, "You are henceforth and forever *Darkling*, and you are welcome here."

The animal's eye looked into me and through me, saw my fears and doubts and knew that I adored him.

62

To the Other I Am Becoming,

Darkling aided the process.

As my children and Nightheart and Bloodfire and I continued towards The Black Mountains, I would, at least once a day, coax Darkling into joining me on a stroll away from camp. He would follow at my heels; something in his innocence and his inchoate mystery lifted my spirits, heightened my sensitivity. With him so close, I was often overcome with the beauty of The Empty Too Much.

I felt and saw and sensed that which I hadn't before: the mad wind's leopard cry, the thirsty silence of the sand as it drank our steps, the delicious visual experience of mirages rippling ahead like small rain-patches in a shower. And, above all, moments of shimmering calm.

And when those moments passed, the sun clanging with light and heat. Together as we were, I found myself conjuring up some pressing question and waiting for the silent answer of the distant darkness to arrive. And I would wish that Salmaya could see Darkling. I would think of her and lost yesterdays.

I began to understand that The Empty Too Much was filled with a great, unconquerable spirit, and that Darkling was like the faith that tends first light and like the hidden music that shapes each day. With Darkling I never experienced an erosion of hope in the hour of shadows.

The forgotten comfort of the unknowable would descend upon us like moonlight through a scudding of clouds. In the rock formations we strolled by I would imagine the doors of the

gods ajar invitingly. I would hear the sounds of strange birds—
they would bubble up from my heart. And always out there
to the west The Black Mountains and the vague, mystifying
promise of The People of the Wild. I often wished that I could
imitate the gods and lay my arm lovingly over those dark and
tender curves of rock and rugged majesty.

Heading back to camp, I would think to myself: *There is a
power here that grips the mind.*

I was convinced that Darkling understood.

63

To the Powers That Be Everywhere,

It seems to me that the mad too often come at one too boldly, and that's how Piro Seghers returned; the late afternoon sun one day a surrealistic ball of fire so intense it appeared to be falling directly upon our camp.

Carrying a water cask filled with something other than water, he stopped two hundred paces or so out and beckoned me. I knew that entering his space would end in shock.

I was right.

Angry, hurt, confused, I strode towards him rehearsing all that I needed to say, but he arrested me with his own words: "Beware the wind that blows the heart to flame."

I suppose he was telling me that it was foolish to be upset with him.

"We've had a difficult time," I said, choking on the understatement.

Waving off my comment, he pointed to the cask.

"I did what I had to do. I had to square up things."

I crouched down with him over the cask, and when he opened it I cringed.

Blood of the gods save us!

There were the severed heads of three men.

I looked into the face of Seghers and then into the faces of the decomposing heads.

"Hunters?"

Seghers nodded.

"Help put up a warning for others like them," he said.

Puzzled, I shook my head. Black flies buzzed with impunity over and into the eyes and mouths of each head. It was a horrifying trio. I found it hard to believe that Seghers could be so calm.

What he meant by warning was a placement of the severed heads there in the sand some distance from our camp. While I positioned each head, he drove a stake through it. When finished, we rose and stepped back as if to marvel at our achievement. It was a most macabre sight.

I felt sickened.

"Does this satisfy your revenge?" I said, my jaw tight. "You get some madness out of your system?"

He sneered at me.

"They did not deserve to live."

Back at camp he seemed glad to see my children, and he was especially glad to see Nightheart and, for that matter, Bloodfire as well. I introduced him to Darkling.

Seghers eyed him appreciatively and muttered, "He's a wonder. A veritable wonder."

Naturally I told him everything that had happened to us since he had vanished on his mission. He had heard of The Hungry Girl, and he knew her lover. He praised my courage. He told my children that he was proud of them. He was confident that we could make it to The Black Mountains. All would be well.

I wanted to believe him.

Late that night, he and I sat up by the fire, as was our former custom, and drank tea as the evening winds played with the flames. Some of my anger at him had been allayed. I found myself needing to talk about my children.

"Sometimes," I said, "Gela can call forth roses from the flatbread we bake."

Seghers nodded.

"She, too, is a wonder," he said.

I told him of my strange bond with Darkling.

He did not seem surprised by it.

"We can't see anything unless we, ourselves, enter into it," he said. "You have entered the animal mystery of that colt and he has entered yours."

Our conversation went nowhere and everywhere.

I had to admit to myself that I was mostly glad Seghers had returned.

He shared with me that while stalking the Hunters he had many weird and yet somehow hopeful dreams.

One of the worst things, he said, is to have dreams without enough sun to let them ripen.

I chuckled at something impenetrable in his words, and then I said, "I live to see that my children reach The People of the Wild, but what else am I looking for? What else am I waiting for?"

He squinted up at the star-flecked night, and the murmured, "For some unseen alternative *other* to possibly arrive."

"Possibly? Why do you say that?"

"Because of the inscrutable. Always the inscrutable," he said, nodding. "And, as well, the realization that there remains something within you that may rise to support you." He paused. "We are all servants to primal forms that unfold in timeless ways."

"Do these forms truly speak to us?" I wondered, my voice soft and filled with doubt.

"Yes," he said. "Primordial forms, primordial images—and when they speak, they speak with a thousand voices."

He alluded to the realm of the ever-enduring. He suggested that we were nearing a point where we could call upon beneficent forces endemic to The Empty Too Much.

"Be wary wise," he said.

Suddenly the only image in my thoughts was that of the trio of heads.

"Why did you kill the Hunters?"

Tossing away the last sip of his tea, he said, "Because the gods asked me to."

My mind was fuzzy. I shivered.

"Are we truly on the way?"

"Yes. On the way to the unfathomable—the divine place of the gods."

"So *this* is the way of the gods?

"No. It is *your* way. *Your* task. Not *mine*."

"And we won't get lost?"

Seghers poked at the fire with the blade of his long knife. "We are approaching a place between maps and between the gods who have fled and those who have not yet arrived."

"Have we reached the Point of No Return? I said.

Seghers smiled, but no flames flickered in his eyes. It was a question I would have to live.

Then, from his backpack he pulled free a clean, white skull. It startled me as he knew it would.

"Another one of the Hunters?" I asked.

"No," he responded. He paused some for dramatic effect. "This is my father. My confessor."

64

To the Image of Confessors,

Sometimes as we journey we lean into a gale of stillness.

I think about the dreams of the dead. I think about what sleeps in the forgotten.

After breakfast the next morning I was breaking down our tent when I heard my children screaming. When I ran to where they were, Seghers held me back. He was looking down at a large red viper.

"This is a bad omen," he exclaimed.

I pulled my children a safe distance from the reptile, and then I saw what had provoked the words of Seghers: quite probably a small bird had been swallowed. The lump of it bulged into view halfway down the body of its predator. With his knife, Seghers sliced off the head of the viper, and before I could stop them, my children surged forward. Gela grasped the headless snake and shook it until the bloodied bird slithered free.

It was clearly dead.

Gela wailed. Simeo prayed. Forg wheezed as if he couldn't breathe.

I looked at Seghers.

"Don't try to stop her," he said.

I saw then that he was referring to Gela who cupped the bird in her tiny hands and began blowing saliva bubbles onto it. After no more than a minute, the bird shuddered. Then jerked its wings. Then staggered to its feet. Then seemed to eye Gela before tentatively flapping its wings a few seconds.

Then a hopping attempt at flight.

Then success!

My children cheered and clapped.

Seghers stared off at the sky.

A bad omen, he murmured.

In The Empty Too Much one hears a darker whispering that death—or near death—utters. Even if one stops up his ears, he can't keep from hearing it. Of course, I wanted to know what more Seghers had to say about the omen of the viper and the bird, but I decided, as was usual with me, not to pursue. Nor did I probe into the bizarre mystery of the skull he claimed was his father's. Had Seghers made that up to unsettle me?

When my children had calmed down and we had commenced a new day of our trek, I stayed close to Darkling and Nightheart and thought about how, in The Empty Too Much, one never loses a longing for the never-known. One never ceases to see a prophetic translucence in the sky.

As another twilight greeted us, we were all tired. Sleep was welcome. I did notice that Seghers sat up somewhat later than was his custom; he held the skull with both hands and studied the face of it. I could see his lips moving. I could imagine that he was confessing something, but what, I had no idea.

During the night I was drawn away.

I made a very foolish choice.

It was the cry of a young woman—or so I believed. No one else apparently heard it. It seemed to come from somewhere west of us, less than a mile. I rose and began to walk in that direction; Darkling made an effort to follow, but I swatted at him to stay in camp, which he did.

I sought, until the approach of dawn, to find the source of that siren voice, but I never located it.

By the time the winds began to shriek, I had thoroughly lost my way.

Those winds fell upon me like a pack of demons, but the noise that issued from them was not a howl, it was a song—a devilish dirge. The river of blowing sand was singing. I recalled Seghers saying that there was no satisfactory explanation of the mechanism by which the sounds in a sandstorm are produced.

Survival was all that mattered. Pressing myself as tightly against a whaleback dune as possible, I had no other option but to wait out the fury.

One day the winds call. The sand obeys. That said it all.

And the voice of Seghers out of memory: '*Each grain of sand waits. For them, patience is everything.*'

Then the booming. A beyond improbable sound—loud, vibrant, ceaseless—a cannonade.

It gripped my soul.

And then the inexplicable sensation of hearing bells tolling underground, beneath my hapless, vulnerable monastery of safety.

This will be my grave.

I felt as hollow as a blade of straw.

I would never see my children again.

Minutes seemed to become hours.

The turbulent, endless flow of wind and sand hurrying nowhere.

It lulled me.

The sleep of death crept towards me one grain at a time.

Waiting, waiting, waiting for it to arrive.

Waiting becoming another of the human senses, the only one capable of connecting with what happened next: the ever-lessening of the wind.

A hushing of the sand.

Then a suspension of every sense organ.

Was I dead?

What was this light?

I waited longer.

Waited until I could feel my heart beating.

With all the energy I could muster, I scrambled out from under a heavy coat of dust and sand, realizing in an almost comically absurd moment that I had become my own dune.

I shook my head. Blinked at the darkness passing.

I was alive in a ragged rush of breath.

And I was not alone.

I heard the stamp of a small hoof.

A weak, yet insistent whinny.
Then the eyes of Darkling fixed upon me.
Eyes that definitely seemed to speak.
'I have come to take you back.'

65

To a Bond I Will Never Understand,

In the end, Nightheart understood what must come to pass.

He mysteriously left our camp at a knowing trot. He did not respond to Seghers when he called out for him to return.

This was our situation.

Darkling had stopped eating the grass and grain we offered. The prayers and chants of my children were not responded to by the gods.

Seghers walked away from the helpless colt. The poor little animal, so desperate for mother's milk, refused to even try to get to his feet.

I went to him and embraced him.

I felt as if I were losing part of myself, an irreplaceable part.

We must leave him, said Seghers.

But I couldn't accept that.

I pleaded for time.

We agonized our way through the daylight hours.

At twilight, Nightheart returned with an answer.

The nostrils of the zebra mare flared at the sight of Darkling.

The colt softly nickered.

Struggled to his feet.

We watched.

I like to think that when Darkling began to follow his surrogate mother he turned once to look directly at me, some acknowledgement perhaps of an unknowable relationship, a secret sharing that must, it seems, remain beyond words.

66

To Language When It Fails,

I awoke, my tongue burning with the bile-sharp foretaste of disaster.

My children had taken a turn for the worse. Sand fly bites covered their hands and their faces, blotching red and itching so terribly that each of them cried out pathetically. And, unfortunately, the Wasting continued to bully them as well. Yet, my children, even as they weakened and ceased their cries, never once fully despaired at the approaching thunder of death.

Mid-morning, I looked to Seghers for an answer.

He responded by pointing out to the north of camp, to a small hillock of sand. What I saw kept me from running away from the insane world that lowered upon me like the hand of doom.

It was a cheetah.

I looked then with the right eyes.

It was Tovelmi.

Just as she always was—luminous, hidden in plain sight, a seamless merger of cheetah and young woman and something more. She lived a safe distance from herself. Her selves. I stared at both of her. *What is she thinking? Of emptiness? Or no thoughts at all—present in the glimmer and hot glint of the desert air?*

She was a phantom within a mirage within a memory.

Could I ever be a part of her world?

I wanted to wade into the strong and secret currents of her blood.

I wanted to say something impressive to her, but I felt my

body filling with words that would never become sentences.

A striding parable of care, she entered our camp and went straight to my children. After she had examined them, she asked Seghers for certain items—things in tiny bottles, things she knew he would have: lotions, oils, potions and pastes.

I started a new fire for her.

She heated and mixed her occult brew of the witchery of healing, then applied it to my children before magically sending each one into a deep sleep.

She promised they would be better by sunset.

She left us some dates that she had stashed in her clothing.

Though I longed for her to stay, she told me that she must go. Those eyes of the wind spoke to me, but I could not read the language of them, and so I did not make further effort to keep her with us. I shook her hand, and so did Seghers.

Fifty paces from camp, that beautiful young woman shed her human form and slipped into the otherness of a sleek, spotted cat capable of outrunning anything else that breathed. I could only watch.

Before she became little more than a speck on the horizon, she slowed, padded to a halt, turned and looked back.

Then Seghers filled the moment with surprise.

"Go with her," he said.

"What?"

"Join her. Go and be with her."

"No," I said. "My children need me."

"I'll take care of them. Go. There is a strange need that tethers you to her and her to you. Go. Explore that need."

I believe I was trembling when I clasped his shoulder.

Was I thanking him?

Telling myself that I was being foolish, I began to run after her. I felt the sensation that my pursuit carried with it the possibility of somehow being anointed. By whom? The gods of longing, perhaps? I did not know, and with each footfall I cared less and less that I might be making a mistake.

Cheetah into woman as she watched me approach.

Her smile as lovely as anything else in nature could be.

I reached out for her hand.

And we touched in a different universe.

My thoughts scattered. I wanted to explain. *Explain what?* Instead the words that escaped pointed forward.

"Where will you take me? Where are we going?"

"To *Sangarrah*," she said, her voice a purr of seduction.

The name shivered through me like an arrow.

"What's there?"

I thought I heard her growl ever so softly before she said, "Wildness and beauty. Purgation and grace."

"And what's beyond Sangarrah?"

She smiled as only a woman on the cusp of anticipated pleasure can smile.

"Moments that have never existed," she said.

67

To Passion Fulfilled and Doomed,

The village of Sangarrah was in the belly between ribs of thin, severely angled rock formations, jagged and formidable. As we entered the first dusty, crowded street, I smelled slaughtered animals and camel dung; voices volleyed and buzzed like a hive of insects. At nowhere else in The Empty Too Much had I seen so many people. The throng seemed mostly to be headed in the same direction.

"Where's everyone going?"

Tovelmi was holding my hand as if I were a child. I followed. I could feel tension in her touch.

"To see *Dans el Nitzrisdi Mokbo.*"

It meant *The One Who Inhabits Danger.*

I said nothing more until the flow of eager and excited people swept us forward to an immense, circular pit, twenty feet or so deep. Chattering, betting, calling out with fear and awe in their voices, several hundred expectant souls surrounded the pit. Leaned in. We joined them.

Here is what all of us looked down upon: a lone, muscular, bearded man, naked except for a loincloth made of gray fur—an utterly magnificent individual well over six feet tall with black hair and black eyes. He stood alone, and as we looked on he began to swing a heavy chain around his head as if it were merely a rope. He swung and roared and howled at the mindless yipping and shrieking and growling amassed at his feet.

Well over fifty sizeable hyenas swarmed near him. So

savage were they that the very existence of death would have been news to them.

"Is he insane?" I said.

Tovelmi stared down at the man. I couldn't read her eyes.

When she spoke, it was in a whisper, and I believe that she addressed her words more to herself than to me.

"He is a blood rise of the primal. He is the dead wild of what can never be civilized."

"Has everyone come here to see him be torn to pieces?" I questioned.

She glanced at me with something like pity in her eyes for understanding little or nothing of the unfolding spectacle.

"They're here because they seek catharsis. Purgation. They're here to view a living enactment of grace. And transformation."

Then the crowd morphed. A sound rose that chilled me to the bone: the eagerly meaningless laughter of a pack of hyenas, and that laughter, in turn, triggered the real hyenas in the pit. And then with teeth bared, they, in one surging pack, charged The One Who Inhabits Danger.

I looked away.

I heard the horrid clamor of attack.

I heard the eerie whistle of the swinging chain.

I heard yelps and screams and the breaking and tearing of bones and flesh. I smelled blood and pain. The cacophony seemed to go on for twenty or thirty minutes. All the while, the crowd cheered and chanted; in their response, I also heard single, sinister threads of mocking, hyena laughter.

Until, finally and of a sudden, the dark concert daughtered out to a whimper.

I heard only whispers of awe from the gathered throng.

Tovelmi touched my elbow, a gesture inviting me to look.

I held my breath.

For a moment, I couldn't believe that what I was seeing was possible.

Most of the hyenas were either dead or badly injured; the survivors limped to the walls of the pit, leaving The One Who Inhabits Danger standing free and tall, bitten and scratched, yet very much alive.

I heard Tovelmi mutter, "Watch. Watch closely."

And so I did.

The man tossed the heavy chain aside.

He lifted his arms as if to challenge the sun above.

He cocked his head back, and he howled as if he intended to draw down the moon.

Then, inch by extraordinary inch, the flesh of the man shifted.

And when the transformation had been completed, he stood, inviolate, the largest hyena I could possibly imagine.

The roar of the crowd made the dusty earth beneath my feet literally quake.

68

To Transformation and Beyond,

"Do you want this man," I asked, "this hyena man?"

Low-ceilinged and secretive, its walls covered with depictions of animals and something resembling humans, the cave Tovelmi brought me to possessed an ancient comfort.

She was cutting strips of meat to drape over a spit. The dagger she used was like that of an assassin; the hasp was emerald green. It was a weapon much more designed to dispatch an enemy than to prepare a meal. But a good fire burned. Supper was in the air. I watched her lips move—she almost seemed to be tasting the word *want* as if it were foreign to her. Impatient, I tried to clarify: "I mean, do you *desire* him?"

Ashamed of my jealousy, nevertheless it was there, haunting me like the shadows we cast upon the walls of the cave. I was on the edge of misery. I missed my children. I felt guilt whenever an image of Salmaya ghosted through my thoughts. But I also had to admit that I had feelings for Tovelmi.

She turned and looked at me, a glow to her face and a mysterious triumph in her dark, inextinguishable eyes.

"No," she said, her voice soft yet certain.

We had trekked through a forbidding stretch of desert to reach this cave, pressing through perpetual heat waves that caused the air to heave. The silence of the landscape generated a tremendous sense of diminishment, and it seemed that infinitude and immensity separated us from the instinct that binds one to life.

Now, cave and fire and shadows were companions to our

companionship. We ate without talking further—meat and dates and a sweetened bread. We drank goat's milk laced with honey. Afterwards, Tovelmi spread a camel hair blanket near the flames.

"I need your touch," she said.

The surprise of her words stirred me, and yet I intuited that she needed something else as well, something beyond the sexual. I had been chosen for a task. What it might be, I could not determine. Truth be, when she stripped herself of her robe, and I reached for her naked body, I no longer cared to speculate.

She stopped my advance with her fingers.

Then I felt claws unsheathe where fingertips had been.

She rolled onto the blanket. In a matter of moments young woman gave way to cheetah, the stunning rosettes, black against the grain-gold fur, the fragrance of animal musk, and her stomach white, inviting me to rub.

Her purring filled the cave.

But the spirit of the cheetah could not hold back the woman in her.

Slowly, ever so slowly, as I caressed her, the animal retreated; the body of a desirable human materialized. I moved knowingly into her arms, and only our shadows witnessed the pleasure we shared.

69

To the Imaginary Music of Affection,

We slept much of the following day. We talked and ate and explored the labyrinth that the cave system entailed. Many things fascinated me about Tovelmi, one among them was that I loved watching her start a fire: the way her hands worked as she twisted and spun a stick between her palms over a bird's nest of grass and twigs. And the erotic pursing of her lips as she blew into the infancy of the flame. Her hands also pulled me into the knowing, methodical manner in which she could dig into a den of scorpions and pinch them free without being stung—how she would dangle, between thumb and forefinger, a roasted scorpion over my mouth and laugh softly as I crunched.

I never, though, effaced the reality that she was an exile.

Her tribe had wanted her to stay with them; she had wanted more. Perhaps it was that she felt an all-consuming need to choose between cat and woman. Not being able to choose had left her stranded in a psychic realm she referred to as *The Great Nothing*. I ached for her. I was of no help freeing her from her dilemma.

Did she believe that I could?

Huddled near the fire, we conversed as man and woman; our topics ranged from one end of the universe to the other. The People of the Wild arose as an authentic interest. I wanted to know more about how she viewed these seemingly unknowable entities.

"They have the wrong name," she declared at one point. "They should be called *The People of Awe*." She gazed into my eyes before continuing. "Wonder hasn't died for them. In the sacred confines of The Black Mountains they perceive shapes—they receive stories. When they open the book of the stars each night, they can read personal messages."

The near poetry of her words dizzied me.

"What is the secret?" I beseeched. "I mean, to existence in The Empty Too Much—what is the key?" I almost stuttered with my questions. I paused to shake my head, for everything I said sounded trite and banal.

She took my hand and studied it in the firelight.

I heard her breath catch every so slightly before she said, "One's capacity for pain and suffering. Through suffering we demonstrate to the gods that we are worthy of crossing into other worlds and visiting them."

"What about sacrifice?" I said. "Being in The Empty Too Much has taught me that I'm willing to sacrifice to see that my children get what they need—that they become healed."

"That's not your true quest," she responded.

"What is then?"

A hush accompanied her answer: "Astonishment and awe." She let her words hover just above the flames. Then she stroked my cheek, and, once again, I had the uneasy feeling that she pitied me. "Mozef," she said, "you have not lived."

I suppose it was a bruised ego, a childish sense of hurt, that caused me to get up from the fire and to go out a few feet from the cave. She joined me, hooking an arm through my elbow.

"What happens when we die?" I asked.

She pointed up into the night sky to the overwhelming sight of the universe, and the countless white flecks from one corner of our view to the other.

"We enter the stars," she murmured. "It's our final transformation."

At that moment I felt that I was being led through a portal of revelation into a state of mind or existence beyond the reach of words.

70

To the End of Something,

Here is what occurred on our final day together.

First light, we went to pick flowers. I had to stifle a laugh at how silly and overly romantic it felt to do so, but Tovelmi read my mind and insisted that I did not see the whole of reality. I told her that I had witnessed Seghers pick the same blue flowers as those we gathered in the clefts of rock and sand. She giggled. A girl inside of her ghosted free; only for a moment, however.

Back in the cave, she crushed the tiny petals and directed me to place some of them beneath my tongue. She helped me out of my clothes. She removed her own; we lay on the blanket, and I smiled into the reality of the taste of aphrodisiac. She took the petals from my mouth and put them into hers, chewed and swallowed. Time lost its energy. Every action, every movement took place slowly and precisely. She reached out and lovingly touched the swelling of my desire. I gave myself to her. For an unknowable passing of languorous minutes we were then consumed by an indescribable, emotional and bodily contentment. The shadows in the cave vibrated as if celebrating with us.

Time recovered, yet not with a ticking regularity.

For our noon meal, Tovelmi prepared a most delicious piece of meat, roasting it to perfection. She smiled, pleased to see how greedily I ate it. I apologized for saving none of it for her.

"I have enough courage for what I need to do," she said.

As I shook my head, I felt a hot pool of confusion form in my chest. For whatever reason, I found myself thinking about something I had heard once, a saying: *all great passions end with a misunderstanding.*

"Help me to see what you're doing," I said.

"I'm sharing someone. Her name," she said, as if she ignored my request, "was *Bara houtma nen,* and though she was very young, she was the bravest among our tribe of shapeshifters. She gave her life for us." And there Tovelmi paused, hoping to witness some flash of understanding in my face, my eyes. She leaned closer and whispered, "When she was killed by the Hunters, I saved her heart. Her most courageous heart. For you. Because I knew what you would need."

I reeled back, sickened, wanting to hate her. But I could not.

Vaguely I recalled what Seghers had once predicted.

She handed me her dagger.

"No, please," I said. "Please, please, no."

"You know that I cannot choose," she said, "one mode of existence over the other, and I can longer be two in one."

With that, she assumed a position on all fours. Woman into cheetah became reality in hardly more than the exhalation of a breath. Those startling black eyes steadied themselves deep into mine before she turned and faced the wall, her body defenseless, inviting a final moment.

The pain in my stomach flamed.

I turned away and heaved, emptying my body in a hot, sticky flow of what I had just consumed. I staggered. I tossed the dagger into the fire. Unable to think clearly, I gathered up my clothes and ran from the cave like the coward I was.

The sound of Tovelmi's savage growl of despair echoed through me.

And followed me all the way back to our camp.

71

To All That Is Inevitable,

West, always West towards The Black Mountains, veering from our path only to avoid the poison winds generated by small, yet falteringly active volcanoes. I felt great joy in being back with my children and with Seghers and Nightheart and Bloodfire.

Yet I was haunted by the memory of Tovelmi.

And what I couldn't do for her.

Each passing day I would think that I saw her cheetah self positioned on some distant hillock staring into me. Only a mirage of my fears. *Mirage.* Such an exotic word; so different from *mud* or *dirt.*

I had failed a woman who had gifted me with a rebirth of love.

Or at least passion.

And now, where was she? Out there in that realm she knew as *The Great Nothing?* Living? Dying? Merely existing?

I believed that I would never see her again.

So I turned all of my attention, gave all of my emotional energy to my children.

One morning I knelt before Simeo and asked him how he was.

"Bless you, my Father," he said, his smile beatific. His breath smelled like that of an angel, or so I imagined. My moments near him always seemed to lodge in one impression: that he was older and wiser than me. He showed me through his presence that I didn't know I was lost—in so many ways, lost, and disconnected from myself.

"But are you strong enough to make it to The Black Mountains and The People of Wild?" I said.

"I am," he murmured. "If the fates allow."

I touched his aged cheek, and I nodded.

When I moved around in front of Forg and asked how he was, he pressed a finger onto my lips and shook his head as if to say, "*No questions, please. Our lives are beyond questions.*"

More and more I saw that he had become obsessed with the dead stummie.

"You shouldn't," I say, "feel guilty about what happened. That snake biting you wasn't your fault."

With a grim hardness in his expression, he whispered, "How do you know?"

He had me there. So I scrambled for something, anything to move him forward.

"Please don't lose faith in the future."

He smiled shyly.

"I've never," he said, "had faith in the future—so how would I lose it?"

Everything about him seemed to exclaim: "*We are defined by our needs.*"

I pressed my forehead against his. I was tempted to say that I was sorry, but I knew that Forg was not a boy open to the failure of language. I should have urged him not to dwell upon taking his own life.

And then there was Gela.

Beauty and goodness swimming in her eyes.

"Where do you get your strength?" I said to her.

A woman's smile blossomed on her little girl's face.

"From my wonderful brothers," she said, "and from you, Dear Father."

I lowered my head to choke back the start of tears.

I reached out and gently pressed my hands onto the sides of her head.

"I promise you—I promise you that we will make it to The Black Mountains and to The People of the Wild."

"Oh, Father," she said. "You need not promise that. You see,

I've already been to The Black Mountains. I've already met The People of the Wild—in my thoughts."

I studied the magnificence of her. It warmed my heart to know how much existence would benefit from her presence. At the end of the game of life, she saw only one goal: love.

Like a man doomed, I spent as much time as possible with my children. I tooted on Grinner, and we sang and played games and looked at Salmaya's drawings. We engaged in Mother Touch. And then one evening with the fire dying down, Gela took my hand and said, "Dear Father, we've been wondering about something."

"What is that?"

"About when you went off to be with Tovelmi—do you love her?"

As much as I wanted to deflect her question, as much as I wanted to embrace self-denial, I felt the stab that tells a man he needs to live in the truth.

"Yes," I said, "I love Tovelmi. But she has her own story to write."

Gela's eyes twinkled with secret points of light.

And wisdom and understanding.

72

To the Questions,

"Why do men always disappoint the women in their lives?"

At the voicing of my question, Seghers threw his head back and laughed as heartily as I had ever heard him, leaving me to assume that he read it as a foolish query.

It was late night.

A light wind. Warm. A feast of stars above us. The hideous cries of hyena, the howls of wolves, the distressed barks of wild dogs and the hooting of desert owls stirring up our silence and solitude. We both had downed a good bit of blue wine. And the blaze of our fire was magical.

Lifting one finger as if to pontificate, Seghers sobered momentarily to say, "We can know the *why* … but the *what* is the thing—and that has been exiled into the unknown."

I kicked at the fire.

"That's not an answer. That's just some of your desert gibberish."

He laughed again. He draped an arm over my shoulder as if were old buddies.

"Listen," he said, "women … women *ask too much*. They ask too much."

He shook his head dolefully.

I suddenly recalled that he had said something similar about The People of the Wild.

"But couldn't you say the same about me?" I pressed.

"No, no, no." He lit a cigarette. Puffed twice. Squinted out into the great nothingness and said, "Men are not *askers*. No, no.

My young Mozef, men are *not* askers—they are *takers*."

I smiled to myself.

"Old man," I said, "on certain days your madness releases you, and you stumble upon wisdom. *Takers* not *askers*—yes, that smells of the truth."

"Ah, but wait," he said. "Maybe. Maybe my words of wisdom come not because madness has *released* me, but rather because it causes my mind to burn with a gem-like flame of clarity."

We laughed the soft laughter of reverie.

We looked beyond the firelight into the darkness.

I believe that both of us inwardly shivered at the thought of what tomorrow might bring.

73

To Wind, Sand and Stars,

Twilight turned against Bloodfire.

All day we had seen again the spawn of dunes, vast accumulations moving inexorably, breeding, breeding until our central path towards The Black Mountains was blocked.

It was as if the fertile energies of The Empty Too Much settled in the proliferation of those dunes—and there was something more: booms and gritty squawks that my children delighted in imitating, desirous as they were to bond with the supernatural.

But to me it all proved vaguely disturbing.

Fascinated, yet wary, Seghers spoke as if he were considering human behavior. "The sand," he said, "is in a bad mood."

Bloodfire stomped and honked and showed us his yellow teeth.

Seghers threatened to beat him.

I argued against it.

"What's wrong with our trusty camel?" I said.

Seghers sniffed the air.

"Something's coming," he muttered.

"A storm?"

He shook his head. Spat at the sand and covered the small blot of wetness with his bare foot.

After our supper, I went out to where Nightheart and Bloodfire were tethered. I patted Nightheart's neck and tousled his forelock before going over to Bloodfire where I witnessed the wild flow of his dark, dark eyes. Near panic lodged there.

"Dear fellow," I murmured, "what is it? We need you to help

us get my children where we have to go. We *need* you."

But there was, in every fiber of his camel essence, the shaping of a necessity beyond what I could understand. He literally shuddered in anticipation of what wanted to come.

Before I left him, he did something most unexpected: he lowered his proud, often ill-spirited head and nudged at me, a gesture that felt like affection.

"You're a good camel," I whispered. Then I recalled how he had been cut open to help with the healing of Forg and his viper bite. I looked deep into the abyss of one eye and added, "Thank you, sir."

74

To a Wildness Passing,

During the night, an unusually large pack of wild dogs traced west not far from our camp. They trotted in a sinuous line as if on a military maneuver. Orders and commands and a singleness of purpose charged through them silently and unerringly.

Near dawn Seghers rose and studied the distant black snaking of the dogs. Then he turned his attention to the East. The cast of his expression told me that he was expecting something.

I scrambled up to his side.

"What's coming?" I said.

In a barely audible voice, he said, "Wildness." Then he slapped at my arm and exclaimed, "We've got to tie down Bloodfire, or he'll be soon gone."

"What do you mean?"

But he didn't answer. And I ran behind him to Nightheart and Bloodfire.

"Never mind about Nightheart—he'll stay."

"What's coming?"

"Take Nightheart's rope and loop it on Bloodfire. Get ready to dig in your heels to hold him."

"Seghers, damn your soul, what's coming?"

He glared at me even as he began to pull at Bloodfire. Almost immediately the glare dissolved into a smile.

"Seduction," he said. "Look back over there."

I turned, and when I saw what I saw I felt a warm needling in my throat. In a train of fifteen to twenty magnificent animals, beauty threaded its way near our camp, seemingly following the same path as that of the wild dogs.

"Camels," I whispered to myself in awe.

Never to be domesticated, brown and red beasts, most two-humped but among them several one-humped as well. I remember Seghers speaking of them. He, though, assumed that we would not be rewarded with a sighting.

Wild camels of The Empty Too Much.

"Hang on to Bloodfire," he shouted. "Help me hold him back."

And then I could see it—in the roaring blaze of Bloodfire's eyes—a flaming desire to join them. His distress jangled. He sang out as if he were being attacked by wolves. Nightheart could only look on helplessly as did my children from the safety of the tent.

"He's got the scent of them," said Seghers. "Hold him."

We tried.

But the strength of the beast was too much for us. When he saw that we most certainly could not keep him from tearing away, Seghers gestured for me to cut the ropes.

Free from our grasp, Bloodfire bucked and staggered and stumbled.

A strange bleating issued from the ugly contortion of his lips.

I wheeled around and saw that the wild herd had slowed. They repeated the bizarre call, and Bloodfire began to swish his tail back and forth much more excitedly than I had ever seen.

Seghers shooed him.

"Go on!" he shouted. "Go be what you've never been!"

He wasn't angry. He was merely resigned to the camel following a new trail, becoming a different beast.

I felt hollow and yet somehow glad as I watched Bloodfire race towards the herd. I found myself expecting that he would stop and turn as if to tell us goodbye. But, of course, he did not.

Seghers walked back to camp.

I stayed, standing there beside Nightheart who nickered once softly. When the horizon finally claimed Bloodfire and the wild herd, I thought of Darkling.

Is he well? Growing? Thriving? Moving in his own magical space?
I did not know.
I looked in the direction of Bloodfire's escape.
"May the gods be with you," I whispered.

75

To the Power of Revelation,

In the heat of the day, Tovelmi's comment froze my thoughts. *You have not lived.*

Of all we had talked about and exchanged, those words lodged in my memory, taunting me, haunting me. I suddenly began, as I hadn't fully before, turning them over and over, examining them from every angle.

What did she *mean*?

Most of all, was she right?

My time spent with her in the cave ghosted through me indistinctly. Yes, I realized that she had asked for more than her blood to be shed—she had invited me to release her from her clutch upon namelessness and the endemic torture of a divided self.

I had not been up to the challenge.

Not nearly so.

Yes, perhaps she was right: I had not lived. Not perilously close to the most dangerous edge of life, not livingly. Yes, The Empty Too Much offered threats. I had encountered several of them, but Tovelmi envisioned more. She had wanted to initiate me into that something more.

She had wanted to prepare me for what I would face in the weeks to come.

And now. Now, I had lost her.

My children snapped me back to reality. By evening they were clamoring to have me show them, once again, their mother's drawings. I happily agreed to, but this time a new spacing within reality presented itself. While I believed that I knew Salmaya as well as a man might know his wife, my children ushered me into the realm of revelation.

Salmaya, in the wind and sand of my thoughts, emerged like a missing chapter in a much loved book.

It happened as we were looking at her exquisite drawings of insects, at the intricate details of one set in particular—the trimanoid, eight-legged creatures—and at one drawing I had overlooked.

I heard something like a rush of emotion in Gela's voice when she said, "Father, do you see? Do you see what my brothers and I see?"

The face of a three-in-one entity suddenly leaped out at me.

What fell through me then can only be likened to the calving of an iceberg, an icy birthing of truth over partial truth.

Simeo echoed his sister. So did Forg.

It was a chorus of joy.

Gela's voice tugged at me.

"Do you see? It's our Mother. It's our Mother."

"Yes," I said, barely able to speak, "I see her."

"Oh, Father, she's one of us. Do you see? She's one of us?"

I swallowed hard.

"Yes," I whispered. "I see."

On one of the heads, the unmistakable, yet tiny face of Salmaya.

Before she was separated long ago from her two siblings.

I sat up by our fire long after my happy children had fallen asleep and even after Seghers had smoked his last cigarette following the polishing of his father's skull.

Why hadn't she told me?

Perhaps she had, I reasoned coldly.

Perhaps I hadn't been prepared for the truth.

Revelation plays by its own rules.

76

To Music and Death and Everything In Between,

Another dawn, another breakfast fire.

We had to buy some thorn tree branches from a ragged boy, not more than nine or ten, who passed close to us toting an impossibly heavy-looking sack of wood on his young back. His name was *Aiolo*. He was headed to The Black Mountains to locate a relative he had been told about.

We gave him a bowl of warm porridge, but he declined our invitation to join us as a fellow traveler. We wished him well.

Waiting for my children to waken, I sat with Seghers and we drank hot tea sweetened so thickly that it made one's nostrils burn. I told him what I had learned about Salmaya. He merely nodded.

"Maeleeva said she thought it was so," was his response.

"Why didn't she say as much to me?"

He shrugged. Then he said, "The sky is filled with words we choose not to speak." He shrugged again.

He had the skull out, this time propped between his knees.

"That isn't truly your father's skull, is it?"

"Yes. May the gods cut off my male organ if I lie."

I chuckled.

"How did you come to possess it?"

"First," he said, "answer this: If your father is still living, when did you see him last? If he has passed, what do you now think of him?"

I told Seghers that, yes, he had passed, and as to my thoughts of him, I emphasized that I admired him as a hard worker, a good provider, but that, alas, we were not close. I told him that I thought my mother had been an uncomfortable burden for him.

And so Seghers, seemingly satisfied, began a rambling tale of how his father, a bone picker and, quite probably, a grave robber, as well as an overly passionate lover of desert wine, was apprehended long ago in a filthy village and accused of stealing the bones of a dead child.

"They sentenced him," said Seghers, "and when the sun was at its hottest, they hanged him. Afterwards they dragged him into the desert for the hyenas and vultures and things leprous to the faithful to pick him clean."

"How were you able to locate the bones?"

For more than a minute, Seghers stared into the mirage of his memory.

"Because I witnessed the hanging. I saw them offer his body to the beasts. I was no more than a boy at the time."

"The gods forbid," I muttered. "I'm sorry. I truly am."

He laughed sourly and rubbed the top of the skull.

"Well," he said, "in that same dirty, end of the world village I met a wild musician who possessed a most delicate lyre that had grown onto his arm like a thick stem of roses grafted onto an olive tree, if you can imagine that."

"Your stories," I responded, "always attack verisimilitude."

He swung his fist at me playfully, making certain *not* to land a punch.

Then he said, "I don't remember the musician's name, but he maintained that if I listened to a particular piece of music he alone knew how to play—well, then I would never die. Now he also emphasized that he could only play the piece when he was drunk on blue wine—the wine of immortality."

"So you asked him to play the piece?"

"I did. When he was hopelessly in his cups, that is."

"And now you honestly believe that you can't die?"

Seghers sighed. A full minute passed before he spoke again.

"I'm afraid I do."

I laughed but with no glee. Then rose to wake my children.

So that we might drink the new wine of wind and sun-glistened heat.

77

To Sitting at the Fire Like Ghosts,

Is it true, I wonder, that one day tells its tale to another?

I have learned that the path through every night is narrow.

In parts of The Empty Too Much, birds slip into madness and peck at their shadows until exhaustion sets in just before the death of their winged spirits.

A cold wind blew into our camp this morning—Seghers claimed that it came from the days ahead. More difficulties? I sincerely hope not, for we have survived several of them recently.

I sit here and feed breakfast to my children and think about escaping with our lives. First, from a flash flood that took even Seghers by surprise. We had camped in a dry riverbed one evening. Mean spirited thunder woke us and lightning danced—and then the skies opened. Never have I seen such rain. Segher called it a *viper strangler.*

We just barely scrambled to safety from the defiant raging of a resurrected stream that throbbed and gurgled, shaping itself indifferently and shoving every living thing out of its way. Muddied and chilled, we sought out higher ground. My children, frightened though brave, tittered and chittered to themselves as they recovered.

The surprising downpour seemed to alarm Seghers greatly.

Miles beyond the miracle stream we entered a lake of gypsum, a dry pan that threatened to blind us. Seghers rubbed boneblack around our eyes; he did the same for Nightheart, and he told me and my children stories of the wind swirling in these dusty areas and lifting travelers up and away, never to be seen again.

Whirlwinds performed before our eyes.

Voices spoke from them in a language only the gods could understand.

We came upon the bones of a very tall and unfortunate pilgrim.

Then we spent a full day recovering from the temporary blindness given us by the hellish reflection of sun upon that merciless pan. Our thirst for fresh water knew no bounds.

When we camped that night we could hear the weird crash of rocks beneath us somewhere down in the awful darkness inside The Empty Too Much.

My children trembled, and I held them.

78

To the Beauty Beyond Suffering,

Strangeness sought us out.

The Empty Too Much never allowed us to forget that we were traversing a lost, isolated realm in which one could, on a daily basis, discover mystery and suffering and extreme otherness. We followed an imaginary path towards The Black Mountains where I trusted that The People of the Wild seemingly waited for the arrival of my children. A foolish fantasy perhaps—but one that kept me going.

Paths crossed. Sacred junctions arose and disappeared.

The *locus* of wilderness and passion flowed in our veins.

I was experiencing an especially strong wave of self-pity one glimmeringly hot morning when we encountered *Mkemea nte Hedneo.*

The Woman Beyond a Name.

Or, a slightly different translation: The Woman Who Needs No Name.

She and four strong young men, well-muscled and very black. They told us that they were headed to The Black Mountains. Like my children, *Mkemea nte Hedneo* was locked in a death struggle with the Wasting. She, too, was losing.

The five of them spent most of one day and one night with us.

What astonished me was the devotion of the four young men to The Woman Beyond a Name. With her ensconced in a colorfully canopied bed, fringed and curtained, these young men had carried her for several weeks from some ridiculously distant place. When the curtain was pulled back, we saw her. We met her. She was impossibly old and mortally ill. I was, shamefully, repulsed by her face, spider-webbed as it was with age and pain. Her eyes, however, still possessed a gleam of intelligence and something more—and, oh, how I wish I could capture in words what that trait was. Around her prone figure were mounds of dusty pillows and ragged blankets, and one more thing: a large and most impressive rooster, bright red-orange in color, sporting a stunning comb and razor sharp talons. The bird was tethered to her wrist, and his name was The Awakener.

We shared water and food with them.

We exchanged stories of our travels and our devotions.

I instantly admired the young men, and I believe Seghers did as well, but The Woman Beyond a Name was truly, truly remarkable, for there was, I eventually recognized, a beauty and grace about her that transcended sickness and mortality.

She marveled at my children, and they returned her response.

As darkness thickened and our fire tongued at the stars, my children sat on the edge of her bed and petted The Awakener and conversed with the old woman, not in words, but rather in guttural humming and throat clicks and snatches of sounds I could not possibly duplicate. Or understand.

Together, the old woman and my children touched a level of existence beyond suffering.

79

To the Holiness of the Heart's Embrace,

At dawn, the rooster did not crow. No, instead he sang in an almost human voice.

I noticed that even Seghers was both charmed and enchanted by it, the soothing quality of the bird's notes, the strangely holy effect of them.

They could not stay, of course, for The Woman Beyond a Name needed the attention of The People of the Wild as quickly as possible. She hugged and kissed each of my children, and when she patted my wrist I felt that I had been blessed by some god. Or goddess.

I shook hands with each of the four young men. So did Seghers.

I could barcly swallow as I watched them lift the bed, one man on each corner pole of the configuration, and begin to trot off towards the western horizon. It seemed to me that a new path literally materialized for them from the bowels of the earth. They followed it intuitively, knowingly.

What strong trust inhabited them!

And what an extraordinary woman had passed by!

80

To Places Beyond the Reach of Fear,

Crossing this part of The Empty Too Much, always heading west, gave me the sensation of being beyond remote, beyond substance. Seghers, thankfully, hugged vigilance to his bosom, and thus remained connected to himself.

But he needed a vantage point.

One morning we left my children under the watchful eye of Nightheart and sought the upper reaches of a nearby rock formation, and from there, to the southwest, we saw them clearly.

The jagged, black glister, sharp-toothed, surreal outline of The Black Mountains; they appeared to be composed of rock found nowhere else, or so I imagined.

My breath caught, and I thought to myself: *The People of the Wild are there. Thanks be to the gods—we are almost to our destination.*

A strange, cool air filled my lungs.

And then I noticed that Seghers was frowning as he squinted at something just in front of the mountain range.

"Damn the gods!" he muttered.

"What is it?"

From his pack he pulled a small, thin telescope and extended it. He pressed his eye tightly against the lens. His lips moved angrily. His facial muscles squirmed and flexed.

"What is it?" I asked again.

He lowered the scope slowly. He was looking and thinking. His breathing was shallow, on the edge of dark concern.

Finally he spoke.

"The Writhings."

He handed me the scope. For a moment what I saw seemed oddly impossible: several miles away, the sand was churning up as if something were burrowing under it. Dust and sand splashed up from feverish activity.

"What in the name of the gods is that? What are the Writhings?"

"Come," said Seghers, "we need to head back to the camp. We'll have to veer off north."

"North? You mean leave our path? No. No, we can't do that. We might not have time. My children. We don't know how long they can wait."

"Listen to me," said Seghers. "Several times a year the Writhings migrate across the deeper sands that front The Black Mountains. No one can approach the mountains while those creatures are moving through."

Impatient, he sat me down, and we huddled out of the wind, and he told me about the giant, desert, worm-like creatures that tunnel beneath the sands and feed upon every living thing in their paths, sucking blood and bone and flesh, challenged by no other force.

"You must believe me," he pleaded.

I knew that I had no choice despite how incomprehensible his account sounded.

We stood again and studied the distant panoply of sand and rock. We quaked in the rising heat. The world around us cooked. Dust devils sprang up threateningly between us and the Writhings, and the deadly space separating us from The Black Mountains seemed more hostile than I imagined it could be.

Back at camp, I told my children that we needed to change our route.

They looked deep into my confusion and doubt but did not complain or question. We were running low on food and water, and I feared that the Wasting was clawing with a vengeance at the health and spirit of my children.

Seghers hunkered down with us and spoke knowingly.

"There is a village not far from here," he informed me,

pointing to the northwest. "We'll be able to wait things out."

We packed up and started on our necessary meander.

And I began to become preoccupied with notions of chance and fate and raw destiny.

And I began to pray to myself for a place beyond the reach of fear.

81

To Messages That Cannot Be Spoken,

Early afternoon, during a water break, Seghers whispered to me, "More bad news."

His tone was bleached of color and warmth.

We were entering a cut through between vaulting rock formations. The only water we had come upon was undrinkable. My children were suffering. Even the usually strong Nightheart seemed to be experiencing dehydration.

Seghers and I leaned into the shade of each other.

"How close are we to the village you spoke of?" I inquired.

Shaking his head, Seghers gestured vaguely to the north. Then, through clenched teeth, he responded, "We're being followed."

I glanced around quickly, but he stopped me.

"Who is it? Where are they?"

Looking straight ahead, Seghers spoke under his breath.

"To the east of us—a quarter of a mile, probably less. One of the Hunters, I believe. A young one." He paused, then added, "One who lives only for revenge is what I assume."

"Only one?"

He nodded.

"But he must be ruthless and absolutely unafraid. We have to be wary wise."

Towards evening we camped, built a fire. Seghers seemed to have a dozen pairs of eyes trained in every direction. The thought of one of the Hunters stalking us chilled me through and through.

I made porridge for my children.

They sensed my anxiety, I believe.

Then, as the first stars winked on above us, someone walked into our camp. Seghers seemed especially baffled that anyone could have approached us without our knowing it.

It was the wood-gatherer, Aiolo.

As before, he was dirty and dusty and comically, pathetically ragged, his feet bare, his eyes rimmed in boneblack. Oddly enough, though we had seen him not long ago, he now seemed years older. On his back he carried another large sack of kindling, mostly small, dead branches from thorn trees.

"Did you lose your way?" asked Seghers. "Weren't you going to The Black Mountains?"

When the boy responded, his voice was scratchy, yet strong, almost defiant.

"I had to backtrack. I had a bad feeling. Unfriendly things out there."

Seghers then warned him of the imminent danger of the Writhings, but the boy suddenly adopted an air of unconcern.

We invited him to join us for supper. He accepted. He sat at our fire and shared what water he had, mentioning that a rock pool of fresh water lay north along our route. Again, as before, he did not appear repulsed by my children; in fact, he paid little attention to them. Instead, I found that he studied me—and it gave me an uneasy feeling.

Seghers asked him whether he had seen one of the Hunters.

He replied that he had: "One that's very crazy in the head," he muttered.

"You're not afraid?" I said.

"No," he replied. "I fear nothing. But I'm careful. I know when to avoid what could harm me."

After sharing our meager supper with us, he rose, hefted his load onto his back and headed off into the darkness. We could not convince him to spend the night with us.

He had miles to go.

When the night had claimed his shuffling outlines, I paused within myself, wondering why he had stared at me so intensely, and what I came to understand was that he had a message for me—no, not a message in words—*he himself* was a message.

But, alas, the innate wisdom of his innocent presence escaped me.

He seemed, all in all, a boy who had fallen into the desert from some distant star. He was a living destiny, and it was as if he wanted to share the approach of his fate with me.

Perhaps that fate was to wander homeless forever.

Or until death emerged from beneath our feet to call us in a way that we could not reject.

82

To a Man Known as Zomastinez,

When we arrived at the village of *Nenumi*, I was greeted by a stranger who turned out, in fact, not to be a stranger at all. He was more surprised to see me than I to see him.

"What you have done is extraordinary," he said, shaking my hand and looking into my eyes almost in disbelief.

My memory suddenly cleared like fog upon a lake.

"You're the scholar from The Tavern of the Bones—I remember you."

He bowed slightly.

"Yes. I am *Zomastinez*." He hesitated a moment, and then when he noticed my cart and the hood that covered my children, he added, "And *they* are still with you?"

Standing in the bright, sun-splashed street, I gave him a brief summary of our adventures, ending with why we had come to Nenumi. I punctuated my account with a question of my own: "But why are *you* here?"

He smiled shyly as he fingered a large, beautifully bound, calf hide folio book.

"Come with me," he said, "I want you to meet a most fascinating troupe. I have been following them throughout the realm. I am their chronicler." His smile widened, and he tapped the book.

I then introduced him to Seghers, whom he had heard of, and I gave him the names of my children and brought Nightheart over for him to admire.

Then Zomastinez gestured for us to accompany him into a

sprawling tent as white as the moon on the outside, shadowy and mysterious on the inside. And there we were to meet the Story-Tellers.

83

To the Mysteries of the Teller and His Company,

His name was *Jyrus*.

Truly the strangest, most tantalizing, most bizarre individual I have ever met: older than the echoes of time past, younger than the latest sunset, he was pale and hideously deformed and possessed the most enchanting, spellbinding voice I could imagine. And of the wonder of his star-bursting eyes I cannot begin to describe. A magnificent teller of tales was he.

And his company of aides and disciples proved hardly less arresting. First, there was a beautiful young man, dark-eyed, olive-skinned and tall and thin, sinuous even, whose name in the language of *always* translated as *Rapture*. As the overture to evenings of tales, he played a coiled, brassy instrument I had never seen before—and, oh, what music issued forth from it! The sound that must accompany angels as they sleep or the heavenly spheres as they whirl about the endlessness of space.

Next there was a serpent known as *Hiss*, the rarest kind of spitting cobra, white from nose to tail and frighteningly huge. The role of said snake was as healer, for it was claimed that the spit of Hiss could *unblind* the blind, and its bite could cause the lame to walk and the dead to rise again and breathe the breath of life.

Last, yet certainly not least in importance, was a creature known as *the Ape of the Unending*—but he was called, affectionately, *Uno*—and, indeed, he was an ape, though also, quite obviously, a man as well. His body spoke all and all a resemblance to a chimpanzee, perhaps twice the size, however, of the normal chimp. His face, on the other hand, was as sensitively human as any human's might reasonably be, given a sensitive brow and mouth and black, albeit compassionate eyes. He was such a stunning marvel to look at that one could barely keep from staring at him.

Uno's special talents were reading minds and seeing the future.

In a private area at the rear of the tent, Zomastinez proudly introduced us to each member of this remarkable menagerie, though I believe that Seghers had met them before.

Jyrus shook hands with my children, and then he won their hearts when he untied his brilliant blue robe to reveal his own monstrosities.

From his neck to his upper thigh, his apparitional form showed evidence of a dozen or more lumpish growths—fetuses each one, in various stages of development, with then one in particular more advanced and protruding from his left side—two arms, two legs and a squashed, frog-like head and face.

That entity he referred to lovingly as his *daimon*.

As evening approached, Zomastinez guided us to a front row seating on the ground before a makeshift wooden stage. Candles were lighted. Curiosity seekers in droves began to enter the tent, their expressions buzzing with desire to be entertained or healed or carried beyond themselves.

That night, no one left disappointed.

84

To the Rhapsodist,

A great host of simple listeners, many deformed, most whispering to each other or to themselves as if confessing sins or seducing a loved one. Rapture played a haunting melody as the throng of more than a hundred people was seated. At one point, he stopped his performance to say that his composition was known as *Glimpses of Eternity*.

Most aptly named.

And then the taking of center stage by Jyrus.

Uno growled out for silence.

The crowd obeyed.

Jyrus sipped from a mug of hot coffee.

He surveyed those in attendance before saying, "Friends, I am *not* a poet; I am a *rhapsodist*, meaning that when you inspire me, I shall piece together for you a tale upon a subject that has been treated elsewhere in our realm for more years than anyone can remember."

The crowd then sucked in its breath collectively as Hiss slithered up next to Jyrus and tasted the mood of things with its magnificent tongue. Jyrus reached down and kissed the snake upon its hood—and a second round of fearful in-breathing occurred from the listeners and viewers.

"I shall need help from you in my audience," Jyrus continued, "as well as from my most intimate companion: *daimon*." And with those words he pulled open his blue robe to reveal the monstrous appendage. Gasps ensued. "I shall also need from some volunteer an object, one dear to its owner. So," he continued, "who has a thing to feed my daimon?"

I smiled down at my children. Seghers glanced at me, his eyes twinkling.

Seemingly then from the outer edges of shadow an aging crone, hooded in an ashen gray, glided forward holding a black rock large enough for her to need two hands to carry it. She offered it to Jyrus as if it were a gift of great value. When he received it from her, she scuttled up to him and whispered something no one else could hear.

Jyrus nodded. He lifted the rock up over his head so that we could see it.

It looked to be ordinary, perhaps lava stone or ebony.

Next, Jyrus lowered the rock close to the head and mouth of daimon.

And something passed between daimon and rhapsodist.

"Friends," announced Jyrus, "our tale for this evening is *The Witch of the Everywhere*."

85

To the Necessary Opus,

The incessant demand of life is to tell tales that help us make sense of things.

Such was the vision of Jyrus.

The mysterious rock, he claimed, came from The Cave of Sorrows, the sometimes abode of the witch—the daimon of Jyrus connected with the rock and inspired a telling.

The Witch of the Everywhere flowed from the lips of the Story-Teller as if the tale lived in his veins: it was a love story of sorts centered on a lonely, yet powerful witch who fell in love with an ephemeral sprite who could not bear to face the sun. Believing in her own healing powers and in the salubrious effects of love, The Witch succeeds in coaxing the nameless sprite to the mouth of her cave where she may greet the dawn and thus live a more complete life. But the eagerly meaningful act fails tragically— the Witch then lapses into a profound state of grief in which strange worlds open to her. Jyrus wisely chose not to share her ultimate fate, maintaining—as something of a coda—that the deepest of narrative inevitabilities are incomprehensible.

Listening, I sensed that he was right.

For the rest of the evening we were entertained by the other members of the troupe, including Rapture and his music; some of his works threatened to make us cry; some of his ditties had us smiling from ear to ear. Hiss, weaving as it lifted its body to terrifying heights, performed three acts of healing, spitting into the sightless eyes of two small boys and a peasant woman.

But when Uno closed the show, I was quite moved and

unsettled by his revelation, for he urged Seghers to participate in a brief session of reading the future. My guide complied, though I must admit, he seemed haunted by puzzlement. Uno began then by gesturing for Seghers to bring forth the skull he kept in his pack; somewhat startled, he complied. Taking the skull gently in his hands, Uno leaned over it, peering into it as if it were a crystal ball. He remained that way for an uncomfortable run of minutes, his concentration intense.

When he finally raised his head and met the eyes of Seghers, his lips moved uncertainly. I believe that everyone in the audience sensed that a less than pleasant future had been broadcast from the skull. At that moment Jyrus stepped forward and placed a hand on the shoulder of Seghers.

"Sir, do you wish to hear what Uno has discovered?"

Seghers stiffened. He glanced down at his feet and sorrowfully shook his head. Then, for some reason, he swung his eyes around and stared at me and the children. When he faced Jyrus and Uno again, he whispered, "I've changed my mind. Yes, I want to hear."

Jyrus studied him before moving close to Uno to receive his findings.

Directing his remarks to Seghers as well as to the audience, Jyrus intoned, "This man, friends, has lived under the yoke of a forbidden love for many years, but I'm pleased to tell him and you that the barriers and constraints of this love will be removed."

Applause shattered the moment.

I thought, of course, of Seghers and Maeleeva and wished beyond reason that Uno might be right. However, the blankness on the face of Seghers did not change; he showed no sign of emotional contentment.

Jyrus gestured for the applause to cease.

"Friends, I must tell you that everyone waits for someone in an unknown but familiar and infinite desert. Fate, I must insist, is often indifferent to us—often exacts a price for what happens to us in the future. And thus I must tell you that in the coming days this man will lose his sight and no longer be able to write in the book of his life."

86

To the Strangeness of Jimbra,

For the next four days we traveled with the Story-Tellers stopping at unpromising villages where those thirsting for marvels and miracles made their way. Seghers, still locked in deep thought about Uno's reading of his future, housed himself in virtual silence, essentially the same restless silence of The Empty Too Much. Spiritually bruised, Seghers seemed, at times, to experience a letting go of all that is magical about being alive. I did not know how to help him.

One dusty, hot, early afternoon we reached Jimbra.

In that curious village I listened for loud, imperative, unheard answers emanating from every seller's establishment, from every derelict inhabitant and from every wind-blown and stony street. There was something terribly incomplete about the village. I tried not to think about it, reading instead the ever-changing condition of my children—one day seemingly healthy, the next, showing obvious signs of attack by the Wasting. I just kept wishing that things for them would not be unkind.

But Jimbra greeted visitors with a soul-shrinking repulsiveness.

At its entrance stood a cage covered in white goatskin, and scrawled upon it writing that encouraged one, for a small coin, to witness a *gaetsetua*. A wild man. For some strange reason, I wanted to see it. Or him.

Seghers took my children on ahead to where the Story-Tellers were to perform that evening. A dwarf with a pocked face and a swollen nose collected my money and that of a few others. A foul smell engulfed us as we waited for the unveiling. The dwarf offered a ridiculous spiel about the savagery of the *gaetsetua*. That it had killed and eaten its mother.

And then, with the help of several bystanders, the dwarf threw aside the covering.

My immediate disgust changed rather quickly to sadness. A sadness for humanity or for what passes, on occasion, for humanity.

The wild man was covered in feces. He was naked, his penis erect; he was very hairy with long fingernails and toenails, and the shape of his hairy face was brutish. But he didn't growl or scream or shake the wooden bars of the cage like a beast. No, he whimpered. Like a lost child. I brushed my eyes across him just once. Just once. The dwarf then began to feed the hapless creature from a basket of feces; the wild man eagerly reached through the bars, evidencing a ravenous appetite.

I staggered away.

But I carried with me the horribly detached look in the eyes of the wild man.

Near an open air café, I found Seghers and Nightheart and my children, and there Zomastinez pulled me aside and we talked in the meager shade of a date palm. He chuckled at my disgust. I glanced around and saw many nomads among the stone-paved streets. Had they drifted in from the Everywhere to hear the Story-Tellers? Why Jimbra? The village gave me a troubling sense of life slowly dying or perhaps slowly living—of life caged and hideous and on display.

As I stood with Zomastinez, I thought of Tovelmi.

Of shapes changing. Animal into human. Human into animal.

Of how unknowable love is.

It occurred to me that in a village such as Jimbra the last shape of things might unfold.

"Have you enjoyed being around these men of long sight?"

Zomastinez's question yanked me back to reality.

"The Story-Tellers? Yes. But I think this will be our final day among them. We must cover the remaining distance to The Black Mountains. We must locate The People of the Wild. My children are what matters most."

He acknowledged that his view of The People of the Wild had changed, that he now believed not only that they existed, but also that they truly possessed extraordinary powers. But I sensed that he feared them. Was he trying to warn me?

"What," I asked, "have you heard about dangers between here and our destination? About the Writhings, for example?"

"The Writhings have migrated on," he replied. "However, be wary wise concerning the Sisters of the Barren—they have become desperate."

I assured him that I knew of those women and that they did not fill me with dread.

He shrugged.

"Well," he said, "perhaps you are even more desperate than they are."

Perhaps, indeed, I was.

87

The Child in the Shadow—To Your Elegant Mystery,

By sunset the open space of the café drank in a crowd of seekers.

As always, the music of Rapture was celestial.

The bite of Hiss restored a man's withered arm.

Uno, through Jyrus, told a profoundly grieving woman that her missing daughter would turn up alive and well.

But, of course, the real show—as ever before—was Jyrus giving birth to tales of enchantment or darkness, good or evil, love or hatred. Stories of how things truly exist even if one could not believe what one had heard.

Over the panoply of days, I enjoyed each of his tales, especially *Singing the Winds To Sleep, A Man Made of Sand,* and *The Cave of the Torturers.* However, the best came on that strange night in Jimbra.

It began with Jyrus uttering his necessary question, "Who has a thing to feed my daimon?"

To my surprise, Gela spoke up.

"We—my brothers and I—have a relic. We call it *Mother Touch.*"

"Ah," said Jyrus, "no doubt a bone worthy of worship."

Gela's eyes pleaded with me. I couldn't refuse. I handed Salmaya's finger to the Story-Teller and his daimon.

Jyrus closed his eyes and held it reverently for many seconds, and then he did something that none of us had seen him do before.

He shivered as if experiencing images of great pleasure.

When he opened his eyes, he smiled broadly.

Rapture played something that sounded like the beating wings of angels.

Jyrus leaned towards my children and said, "The name of your story is *The Child in the Shadow*."

It was an astonishing story of patience.

A story of a young woman with a passionate desire to bear a child. But her desire did not find fruition—not in the usual way, and so she waited and did not lose hope and did not let her courage wane.

She was a paragon of patience.

And then one day she gave birth.

At the promised end of day as she walked the main street of her village, her shadow followed her, steadfastly connected to her, and as she smiled upon the phenomenon that each of us has experienced, something happened.

Something walked out of her.

Stepped out of her mid-section.

She froze.

Tears came to her eyes.

It was a child.

Almost real.

The Child in the Shadow.

The one she had waited for, the one that needed her patience to emerge.

A thing made of longing.

88

To Fears That Will Not Die,

Then at dawn we parted from them.

Zomastinez asked whether he might include us in his chronicle of the Story-Tellers. I told him that we would be honored. I looked to Seghers for a seconding of my response. He nodded.

I gave Rapture a hug. He smelled of candles and a perfumed wind.

Uno shook my hand; he sought out my eyes and gave me the most understanding look that I have ever received. He read my mind. He read my future far into whatever may exist beyond. The hint of a smile on his lips suggested that moments of emotional contentment might possibly be in store.

Then Jyrus was there, hunkered down by my children. I knew—and dreaded what was to come next—and he would not allow me to shy from it.

It was a matter of courage.

"Mozef," he said,"your children are ready."

I knelt down to them as well: to Gela, Simeo and Forg.

"What do you think?" I asked them.

Gela smiled.

"Dearest Father, we will obey you. We know and feel your love."

And, as was often the case, the wisdom in her oh, so young voice amazed me.

Simeo and Forg echoed her words—Simeo gently; Forg brusquely.

I rose and stared into the face of Jyrus.

I took a deep breath.

"Yes, let's do it. If the Wasting can be cured here and now ... yes, let it be done."

In all its rare, beautiful and lethal enormity, Hiss slithered up to my children.

Gela said, "Father, I'll go first."

I stood watching on the edge of the abyss of fatherhood. I felt emptier than The Empty Too Much and possessed of more madness than Seghers ever had.

When Gela offered her tiny arm, Hiss reared back, its eyes riveted to the exact spot it needed to bite. With its mouth open, the fangs seemed to load up with venom and situate as fiercely as all the terror that mankind has ever known.

I watched in total disbelief.

Then I felt my tongue tear at its roots.

But the shriek seemed to erupt from beneath my feet.

I heard the word *No* explode and stun the morning air.

Shaken to my bones, ashamed and yet relieved, I realized that the word had risen from the deepest, oldest region of my fears.

I dropped to my knees and extended my arms as far as possible and, trembling out of control, hugged at my children. I did not lessen my grip upon them until I could feel their tiny fingers of love tapping at me with understanding and forgiveness.

Deflected by my cry, Hiss bit into the sand; the honey-colored venom glistened and glimmered, pooled and saturated.

89

To All the Questions That Keep Us Alive,

Why must we trust what is difficult?

As we made our way back into the nameless area fronting The Black Mountains, I sensed that The Empty Too Much never intended anything for us other than a vast unwelcome.

Would The People of the Wild rescue us?

Would my children forgive me?

I mean, not so much with words, but rather this: in their hearts.

I cheered myself only through expecting the immeasurably surprising and not the reasonably inevitable.

Just a man wanting the best for his children—that's all.

Joyous songs for them.

As the sun fisted down upon us, I walked beside Nightheart in his loyal steps as he pulled without complaint the cart in which my children rode. Seghers, more alive in spirit than he had been for several days, lagged back to join us.

"Don't think about what's really out there," he said.

"Isn't it simply inevitable death?" I responded bleakly.

I saw him glance to the north and shake his head. I followed the angle of his looking but saw nothing but sand and rocks.

"Vengeance, dear Mozef—if you can see all the way to the end, then you'll see vengeance and its shadow."

"The Hunter? The young one? Is that it? Is he still following us?"

Wordless, he trudged on deep in thought, deep in anticipation of what he must do.

At our evening fire, each of us commented on how much we missed the Story-Tellers. Obviously inspired by what they had experienced, my children took turns playing the role of Jyrus, spinning their own simple, heartfelt tales: Simeo told a story about angels; Forg gloomily whispered a sad one of sacrifice and death; Gela, yes, Gela—to her was left the task of narrating a charming tale of love as the ultimate assertion of goodness.

Stories gave way to questions.

Forg voiced his in a tone equal parts bitterness and fear.

"What's going to happen to us? Do we have any hope? Are we doomed?"

Then it was Simeo's turn.

Claiming that he had been visited by an ethereal spirit composed of glistening light from some secret source, he asked, "Do such spirits know more than we can know? That spirit presented me with a vision of two of us buried beneath a pile of stones—what does that mean? Is the spirit preparing us for an end that has already been written?"

Gazing into my eyes, Gela smiled lovingly.

"If Simeo's spirit has shown the truth, will you, Dear Father, seek out the one left behind?"

With tears threatening to flood my very being, I pressed myself into their concerns. My voice quavered as I began, not so much to try to answer them, but to share the countless feelings I harbored for them. Some of it, no doubt, was trite and not worthy of them and the haunting maturity and hard realities of their questions. I pressed on, stumbling, stuttering at times, until I emptied it all out: the unspoken, the untold and the secret.

Dawn found us far from tongueless.

And closer than our hearts had ever been.

90

To the Art of Sacrifice,

The end of another day, and I sit alone at our dying fire. What happened hours ago has left me shivering. It feels as if the stars themselves are showering ice down upon me.

My children stir in and out of sleep. They are not well.

Nightmares must be their companions.

Seghers has ridden off upon Nightheart to be alone, or so I suppose. Perhaps he is scouting out the location of the Hunter who seems bent upon revenge. Perhaps he is seeking water. Perhaps he has put the day behind him.

I long for the touch of Salmaya.

I long, as well, for the touch of Tovelmi.

I think back to dawn, combing those early moments of waking for signs that horror would visit us. What I recall is that over our first cup of tea Seghers mused, "Could it be that facing death is like looking into the glare of the sun?"

His question surprised me.

"How," I said, "does a man who believes he cannot die make such a comment? Besides, isn't death more likely an inviolable emptiness that dwarfs even the endless desert?"

Seghers filled one hand with dust and grains of sand and let them sift away as if he were indifferent to them.

"We could think of death as a place we'll all travel to and become lost there—beyond rescue."

I heard a sardonic tone in his remark.

"There is no fear like the fear of death," I followed.

He turned to me, narrowed his eyes and spoke with some intensity.

"But will we *feel* it? Death, I mean—*feel* it as we've never felt anything else?"

I didn't or couldn't answer. Instead, I looked towards The Black Mountains. As we neared them I was shaken by a sense of imminent, glorious rediscovery—but of what? Great peace and solitude, I believed, in the aftermath of my children being healed. It would emerge from the unearthly-of-the-earth, remote, detached and everlasting.

I thought of all we had experienced: terrifying things, precious things, irrecoverable things: grand, wild nights of loneliness and togetherness among the sands—and that most haunting of sensations—that we had chosen to trek through a place from which no one could truly return.

As Seghers poured himself a second cup of tea, he noticed the direction in which I was looking.

"That area in front of The Black Mountains—everyone says it's nameless. Not so."

My interest was roused.

"How then is it known?"

"Men of old called it *Sigberosst Nu Crme* or the Desert of Stolen Dreams."

I whispered the name to myself. It seemed a darkly accurate characterization.

Seghers waved a hand up into the chilly morning air.

"Where we are headed, the night wind passes over this uninhabitable tract of land carrying a shrieking throng of winging, chittering vampire bats bound somewhere for blood."

I almost chuckled.

"Nothing about our journey promises to be easy, does it?"

Seghers laughed, "So true, my friend, so true."

But the threat of winged creatures proved to come from something other than vampire bats. At a small oasis, the last before the final approach to The Black Mountains, we stopped for water and for rest. My children enjoyed the fresh, cool water; even more so, they enjoyed seeing again the wood-carrier, the boy known as Aiolo, who joined us. Once again, he locked eyes with me; then, however, he gave his attention to my children. He sat with them, and they told him about the Story-Tellers.

I confess that, being quite tired, I dozed off.

I awoke to screams.

And the ugly cries of huge, black vultures.

And the sight of Seghers swinging his knife at them.

And of my children trying to seek shelter.

And of Aiolo wielding a thorn tree branch as a weapon in an attempt to protect his small companions.

The wing of one of the attacking birds cracked against the side of my head. I spun to the ground unconscious and stayed that way for several minutes. I came to in time to see a sacrificial horror.

Aiolo, still brandishing his piece of thorn tree, had chased back into the desert, selflessly drawing the vultures away from Seghers and Nightheart and my children. I felt a surge of relief when I saw the birds finally relent, circle in a many-angled round, and head off for other forms of prey.

Aiolo stood out there alone.

I think he must have felt proud.

And then, even as all of us watched, the sand erupted. A predatory, savage orifice opened at the boy's feet, and in hardly more than the blink of an eye he disappeared.

Was swallowed.

Gone.

Seghers shouted for us to hide among the rocks, but it wasn't necessary.

The lone Writhing had satisfied its hunger.

It sank beneath the baking sand and was seen no more.

Unceasing winds erased every sign that a tragedy had occurred.

91

Prelude To a Certain Dawn,

Evening found my children chanting praises in the name of Aiolo, boy of courage, boy of sacrifice.

We had camped in the Desert of Stolen Dreams.

Would *our* dreams be stolen?

In the middle of the night I awoke intensely alert, sensing that something was very wrong. Once I had scrambled out of our tent I saw that Nightheart was securely tethered, but Seghers was not in camp.

What now?

I told myself not to panic. He would return.

Restless, I went ahead and built a fire using clumps of desert thistle. The flames lifted my spirits; hot tea warmed my insides and pushed back at the chill of the night.

I waited.

There, to the west, in dark outline under the stars, were The Black Mountains. They seemed more than a destination; language, however, failed in terms of my finding the words to describe what those mountains represented for me and my children.

Then, like a ghostly rush of feeling, the image of Aiolo haunted my thoughts.

I put down my mug of tea, and I cried soundlessly, the tears gushed from my eyes as if they might never relent. I put my head on my knees and sobbed.

I heard Nightheart nicker.

I snuffled once and wiped my nose on my sleeve.

And a voice said, "You and the ones with you have to pay. I'm here to make it be done."

When I glanced up, at first I saw no one.

"Who's there?"

"Never mind knowing that. Just let me be quick about doing what I've come to do."

It was a young man's voice, slightly high-pitched and tremulous.

I shaded my eyes from the firelight, and there, maybe fifty paces beyond, stood a beggar of a figure, smelly and thin, carrying a rifle seemingly as large as himself.

The young Hunter who had been stalking us.

I stood and raised my hands.

I was frightened, and yet I also, for some reason, felt sorry for him, a homeless orphan of the night on a thankless mission. Because I couldn't think straight, all I managed to mutter was, "Please don't harm my children. They've come so far."

Even to my ears, those words made no real sense.

He stepped a few paces closer, raised his rifle and cleared his throat.

"Well, you see, harming is the only thing I'm out here to do."

"Wouldn't it be enough," I said, "if you would just do me in? Not harm my children—just me?"

His eyes filled with suspicion and doubt, he glanced around.

"Where's that other one? The one that butchered some of the ones I'm with?"

No sooner had he offered those words than I caught a slithering of shadow.

I heard the young man's breath escape in a *whump*.

I saw the blade of a long knife jut out a few inches above his heart.

Saw the spewing of blood.

Saw the young man lower his rifle.

Saw him drop slowly to his knees as if he were about to pray to some unknown god.

Saw Seghers looming behind him. Trembling. Nearly out of breath.

Satisfied.

92

To the End of Something,

I insisted that we bury the young man.

Reluctantly, Seghers helped.

For reasons that escape me, I was angry with my guide and companion; I looked at him and said, "I don't want us to stop moving today until we're ready to walk up into those mountains. We're coming to the end. We've been on this journey long enough."

With another full day of trekking, we made it.

Late afternoon, we camped in the shadows of the vaulting black rock. Though weakened, my children sang out and celebrated. I played Grinner. But Seghers drew a long face.

"You think I'm a coward, Mozef? Do you? For stabbing our enemy in the back?"

I said, "I don't know what I think."

And that was the truth.

Hands on his hips, Seghers seemed weary.

"Well, so it is. But another time has arrived," he said.

"What is that?"

He cupped my shoulders with his hands and looked into my face as if it were a bottomless cistern.

"Time for Seghers and Nightheart to leave you. We've completed our task. The People of the Wild must be waiting near the top of that rock trail."

He pointed to a narrow, steeply angled line that cut along the face of the formation.

I think I must have gasped. The end had to come—I knew

that, of course, but I hadn't prepared myself for it. How does one get ready for difficult goodbyes?

"Thank you," I whispered.

Every other word I needed to say died.

Seghers took Nightheart's rope and led him to where my children were finishing their supper.

"Brave little ones," said Seghers, "you are as miraculous and precious as all the stars in the heavens. Is not that true, Nightheart?"

I watched as if stunned while Seghers hunkered down and gave each child a hug and a kiss: Gela, Simeo and Forg. Each stroked his old, mad face. They touched Nightheart's muzzle. They chanted something, a thanksgiving known only to them, though Seghers seemed to understand. He gave every indication that he was very pleased.

I finally shook free of my muteness, grasped his hands and said, "Will you go back?"

Seghers smiled.

"Back to where?"

I nodded.

I wanted to mention Uno's reading of the future. Was Seghers concerned about what the ape man had shared with him? But I decided not to.

Then I embraced him.

Then I rubbed my face against Nightheart's neck.

"We'll always be in your debt," I said to the both of them. "Thank you for everything."

It seemed much too little to say.

He smiled at me.

"Look there," he said, his eyes glinting, knowing that there was something I was not aware of. He pointed once again to the trail.

I blinked.

"What?" I said.

Then I saw her.

Tovelmi.

High on a flat jutting of rock.

Young incomparable woman.

Then, like mist fading, young woman into cheetah. Waiting?

93

A Promise to Keep,

My children and I spent the night at the base of the mountain.

We missed Seghers and Nightheart and readily admitted it to each other, and yet our guide and his trusty wild ass had completed the job we had asked of them. Seghers needed to re-enter his life. Nightheart was like the man's animal self.

At first light Salmaya rose arrestingly in my thoughts as I woke my children and tended to their needs. I had kept my promise to my wife—I had gone into The Empty Too Much to search for the healing that our children so desperately needed. We had reached The Black Mountains. We needed now to locate The People of the Wild.

Before the sun boiled up too hotly, we began trekking up the trail; my children sang—well, Gela and Simeo did—and my heart pumped forcefully with expectations. I didn't know for sure that The People of the Wild would even welcome us. I simply trusted that they would.

Then, up ahead, I saw her again.

Tovelmi.

Lovely young woman.

A few hundred paces away at most. Excited, I called up to her again and again, but she did not respond. So, with determined steps, I trudged on, pulling my children's cart until we were within a stone's throw of her.

I called again.

But with the sound of my voice she transformed—woman into cheetah—and with breathtaking agility made her way down the treacherously steep face of the mountain and disappeared.

My heart sank.

Gela's voice cut through my disappointment.

"Father, Father, look at the strange man!"

Yes, there on flat surface of the trail's end, someone waited, someone I had seen before. He stood at the entrance to a relatively small orifice leading into a cave, or so I supposed; he beckoned us on.

It was the lizard man from outside The Tavern of the Bones.

"Through here," he said, pointing into the dark opening, "you'll find a path to The People of the Wild."

I thanked him profusely. I wanted to embrace him, but he seemed not to want to be touched. I told him how his recommendation of Seghers as a guide had worked out well. He seemed pleased.

My children and I were almost delirious as we pressed into the opening. But when I turned to once again thank the man he was not there—only a scattering of large lizards occupied his former space. I never even learned the man's name.

94

To the People of the Wild,

I sense that days have passed—how many I can't be certain—and the details of what has occurred have surprisingly blurred. Could it be that the plan of The People of the Wild is for it to be so?

Here I'll record what stays with me about our fateful encounter with these mysterious beings. We followed the cave's pitch black tunnel for a short distance. Then we halted abruptly for two reasons: first, the rising of a ghostly light and, second, the sound of a stream rushing close to our feet—a stream *within* the mountain.

And then we saw them. A dozen or more.

Figures a hazy violet in color surfacing from that stream, and yet we soon learned that it was not a stream of water at all. Rather it was the mystical flow of the mountain itself, a *dark energy* that they referred to as *Pilehme vutnze*. It was an utterly inexplicable phenomenon.

The People of the Wild approached.

Beyond their unusual coloring, they seemed to be underwater spirits—even though there was no water—a crazy admixture of seal and mermaid, yet manifestly human as well. Androgynous, I believe.

An incredibly gentle soul named *Brechlezera* formally greeted us with a reassuring wave of what seemed as much flippers as arms. He (I use that pronoun for the sake of convenience only) was apparently a leader of sorts. He knew who we were and why we had come.

What I remember next is asking, "What's going to happen now?"

"Your children will decide."

"Oh, but they can't."

"Yes," he said softly. "They can. In fact, it is likely they already have."

I turned to my children as if for affirmation. Though they were weak, I saw a glint in the eyes of Gela and Simeo that said, *All will be well. Don't worry.*

Before they were taken away, my children had a request: for me to play Grinner one last time. I nervously did. Even Forg offered a grudging smile in response to my attempt. Then I seem to recall that *Brechlezera* approached and placed his flippers on my temples.

Dark energy flowed through me.

Specks of violet light.

He cast a spell over me.

Put me in a trance.

I became oblivious to the fact that I didn't know when I might see my children again.

95

Waiting For What Wants To Come,

When I roused, I found myself in a windowless room of damp rock lit with small torches. One of The People of the Wild was there with food and a tart wine.

He (again, my pronoun choice on a whim) claimed that he was of the family of *Brechlezera*; however, I honestly didn't understand what the term *family* meant for these curious beings. While he may have mentioned his name, I don't recall it.

I asked immediately about my children.

"They are well," he said. "The Wasting no longer afflicts them."

I was pleased more than I could say.

"Where are they? When may I see them?"

His hesitation troubled me.

"Not yet."

"Why not?"

"Because they need … time."

He said the word *time* as if it were not a concept he was comfortable alluding to.

"Time for what? What's wrong?"

"They are considering whom they must become."

"I don't understand. They're my children. They are who they are."

Anger and frustration bubbled up within me.

"Please," he said, his tone filled with an unmistakable need to reassure me. He sat with me, a deeply patient soul, one who knew secrets and protected them. "Please come and experience some light. You have been in darkness for longer than is good for you."

He then led me out of the inner realm to what must have been the other side of the mountain, to a vantage point overlooking a barren stretch of sand and loose rock.

"This," he said, "is The Land Where the Dead Wind Speaks. I have just come from there on a mission to retrieve the bodies of several foolish adventurers. Our people succeeded in bringing the younger ones back to life. But the apparent leader, an older man, was beyond our help."

A curious discomfort cobwebbed across my chest.

Cautiously I said, "I met an older man once who wanted to send younger men into that realm to search for Men of Never. He didn't feel able to come here himself, though."

Do you recall the man's name?

"Yes," I said, "it was *Treml*."

My utterance was met with a frown.

"Oh, then, I am very sorry. Your acquaintance passed into transition. We could not save him."

I thought instantly of Maeleeva.

Then, of course, I thought of Seghers.

I recalled Uno's reading of his future and something vague about barriers to forbidden love being removed.

The sunlight bore down upon me. I had to close my eyes and turn my face away from the scene.

"Come," said my companion, "let us go back inside. Very soon now Brechlezera will have some important news for you regarding your children."

"What is it? Please don't make me wait. I must know. I must see them."

But the man—if man indeed—young in the face, deflected my pleadings.

He merely issued a soft bark, like that of a seal, and I instantly lapsed once again into a trance.

96

They Call It Home,

In that trance I possessed no sense of past or future, only an endless *now* during which I began to enjoy sitting on the rocks within the mountain and watching the dark energy flow by at my feet, watching it glitter and glimmer. It rushed along in a stream perhaps five paces across, and I imagined that I saw ebony-colored, fish-like entities swimming against the flow, and I found myself wanting to have the right equipment to catch some of those entities.

On occasion, members of The People of the Wild would jump into the swift purling of energy; they appeared to be bathing in it, but when I showed an interest in doing the same, they warned me against it.

I was never to enter it.

But they could not prevent me from being obsessed with it.

Endless questions rose as I stared at its surreal movement.

Where did this energy originate?

Who created it? The gods?

Did it have an end?

Did it flow into a great sea of dark energy somewhere at the end of time?

Was dark energy used to heal?

Was it used for transformation?

I often remained so enchanted by the weird phenomenon that I would forget to eat or drink or even sleep.

It was in one of those deep modes of contemplation that I

suddenly heard a voice say, "Do you know why we are called *The People of the Wild*?"

I turned to see the bemused face of Brechlezera.

"No," I said. "Is it simply that this part of The Empty Too Much is a wild and inhospitable wilderness?"

He shook his head and pointed at the flow of dark energy.

"*That* is *the Wild*. It is our everything—our gestation and birthing. Our beginning and, one day, will be our end, though our minds can't quite grasp that."

I stood and looked at him, the smooth, seal-like features of his cheeks and the black pools of his eyes. I couldn't siphon off the desperation in my voice.

"I want to see my children. Now. I must see them. I've waited long enough."

"You shall, then. Come along."

Surprised and pleased, I followed him out into the light, and we began a slow descent down a new trail. A hundred or so paces down it, he halted.

"Prepare yourself for the decision your children have made."

"What do you mean? Please. Please tell me."

He then merely gestured for me to continue walking with him. Lower and lower, and the rock blacker, more volcanic and rugged than before. At last we reached what appeared to be a caldera that opened upon a flat expanse of sand and a few unpromising pools of water.

Small creatures moved around on the surface of the area. From a distance they looked like insects.

I heard Brechlezera say, "They have made a good choice. Your children—they have found their home."

The confusion that arose in my thoughts dizzied me.

"What are you talking about?"

From beneath his long robe he lifted free the slender tube of a telescope. He looked through it; adjusted it and then handed it to me, showing precisely where I should aim it.

Up from my lungs and into my throat a growl of disbelief gathered.

I saw dozens and dozens of trimanoids—three-in-ones—adult entities as well as children. I could not speak. I could not.

Then my companion drew the scope slightly to the right, to a sloping wall of rock out of the direct rays of the sun.

Under my breath, with tears rising I whispered, "Those are mine. My children."

There they were, near an adult trimanoid, seemingly listening to instructions of some kind.

Gela, Simeo and Forg.

Words burst from me: "I have to see them. I have to make them change their minds."

"No," said Brechlezera. "They have thought this all through. It is best. In fact, if in your mind you do not give them your blessing it will cause them to have doubts. Grave doubts."

I wailed loud enough for the entities below to hear me.

I felt my knees begin to buckle.

Had Brechlezera not held me up, I would have fainted.

I do not even remember his leading me back up the trail and into the mountain.

I had lost my precious children.

97

Dark Night of My Soul,

A much deeper trance this time.

In my fellowship with darkness, I began to sense that I was being watched. When my eyes adjusted to the cave-like blackness, I glanced around and saw them: two red eyes.

The eyes of my personal demon.

Somehow I knew it to be the case.

I knew, as well, that I was in for hellish torture from him.

Looking back, I believe the anguish was spread out over a number of days, and the worst of it sprang from my fear of being *touched* by my demon, whose body I never got to see clearly. But he knew that I was terrified of his making physical contact with me—and he played upon that terror with the consummate skill of a musician.

Every demon is terrifying.

But none more terrifying than a personal demon.

Then, beyond cause and effect, a moment arrived in which I was released.

I sat upon a rock peering at the flow of dark energy.

I was suddenly cageless.

Brechlezera approached me.

His only words, uttered with profound sadness, were these: "There has been a change."

At first, I only felt more confusion.

Moments later, I felt relieved. I sensed that the change alluded to must relate to my children. I remember being escorted out on the side of the mountain from which I had entered the realm of

The People of the Wild. I remember Brechlezera gently pushing me out through a narrow entrance into the light.

As my eyes adjusted to the sun, I heard a familiar voice.

"Mozef, they have left tracks. We must follow."

I blinked.

Standing there, smiling wisely and holding a lead rope looped over the neck of Nightheart, was Seghers.

I stumbled into his arms.

98

Tracks That Lead Nowhere and Everywhere,

I knew those tiny feet.

But where were they leading me?

Down to the base of The Black Mountains we trekked. Puzzlement seized Seghers as firmly as it did me. The tracks, those beautiful, meaningful tracks, swung away to the north.

"They are going to the caves," said Seghers.

I couldn't wait to see them. To embrace them.

To have them again. My children.

Often along the way I would stop and lean over to brush my fingertips across those tracks, feeling elation with the contact.

"Where are they taking us?" I asked again and again.

Then a moment in which Seghers quite suddenly stopped. We had followed the tracks for nearly an hour when he hunkered down. We saw several other footprints.

Then hideously dark stains in the sand.

Seghers hissed, "Oh, damn the gods!"

"What is it? What is it?" I shouted.

An audible click issued from the throat of Seghers. He stood and studied the footprints as they angled back to the east.

With an eerie calmness he said, "They were ambushed."

My mind went blank. My emotions froze.

A voice up ahead of us rode upon a slight breeze.

"You are too late. I'm sorry. So very sorry, but you are too late."

It was Tovelmi.

The Girl With the Eyes of the Wind.

"What happened here?" said Seghers.

"Come to my cave," she said, "and I'll explain."

I was in such a state of shock that I could barely walk. Tovelmi took my hand. She guided us up into the nearby rock formation where she had claimed a small cave as her shelter.

And there on the floor of the cave I saw two small bodies wrapped in milky white goatskin.

I cried out until my voice tore, and I entered a mysterious state—the heart of a distant stillness—and I was alone there with my companions and my grief.

99

To the Ones Left Behind,

We dug shallow graves for Simeo and Forg.

I was numb beyond tears.

Seghers and Tovelmi offered every ounce of comforting they could.

I asked them to help me erect a chorten, a small burial monument for my two sons. Each construction consisted of flat rocks piled one on top of another. When we had completed them, Seghers and Tovelmi stepped away in order that I might have a moment or two of closure.

I thought of Salmaya.

And even more so, I thought of Gela.

What in this desolate, terrifying world had happened to her?

I touched each chorten with my fingertips and I spoke very softly.

"My sons, I promise that I will find Gela. I promise. Know that in my thoughts, every second of every day, you will live, you will live forever, and I will always, always, always love you."

Around a fire that evening Tovelmi described what she believed to have occurred.

"It was the Sisters of the Barren," she began, a renegade branch of them, and they knew that they could save only one of your children. They wanted the girl. They wanted Gela."

I found that I could only listen with half my attention.

Tovelmi went on to speculate that my children wanted me to follow their tracks to her cave. Through some kind of near supernatural sensitivity, they knew where she was. They believed that I needed her. They were willing to risk their lives. They believed in sacrifice if that's what it would take.

When Tovelmi finished, Seghers asked, "Where might the child be? Where do you think they are going with her?"

She shook her head.

Later I summoned an unconvincing bit of speech and directed it to her.

"Will you be staying?"

Cheetah eyes looked through me.

"I must always be going," she said. "One day you will accept that."

Part of me wanted to head out into the night to find the Sisters of the Barren to rescue Gela, but Seghers cautioned me to be sensible.

"Rest first," he said. "Tomorrow we'll begin. Tomorrow, after sleep has given you strength and clarity."

100

To What Must Be Followed,

I was disappointed, and yet I was not surprised when at first light I woke to find that Tovelmi had left.

I must always be going.

No, for now, I was not capable of understanding what her life required.

Seghers had been up tending to Nightheart when he called for me to join him just outside the cave.

"They have returned," he said, pointing down at the base of the rock formation.

Yes. The Sisters of the Barren.

But what did it mean?

Were they taunting us? Taunting me?

My heart rose into my throat when I saw that one woman carried a child; it was wrapped in a blanket and she pressed it protectively to her body.

I knew that it was Gela.

As I started a mad dash to retrieve her, Seghers stopped me.

"No, wait, I'll go. I'll take Nightheart."

I watched him clamber to the bottom, to the open area where the Sisters of the Barren made no attempt to flee. Seghers had his knife drawn. And then I could wait no longer. I bounded over the rocks, shouting, damning the kidnappers, blood in my voice.

I slowed, however, when one the women, seeing the rapid approach of Seghers, raised one hand to her face and made the sign of The Evil Eye. An instant later Seghers stumbled, staggered and fell to his knees.

He had been blinded.

With a laughter like that of hyenas, the Sisters of the Barren triumphantly drifted away.

I called Gela's name.

And heard only the echo of it.

When I had helped Seghers back to the cave, he directed me to take a certain salve from his pack and to apply it to his eyes. We waited an hour or longer but to no avail. His sight did not return. I made a new fire, and he lay by it, bound tightly by both pain and anguish. Then sleep overtook him.

Strange things occurred as he slept.

I was visited by a vision of grief, a haggard woman whom I believe had come to me after the death of Salmaya. Her voice was cold and imperative. *Look into my eyes*, she said. *Don't glance away. I am your grief. I exist only because you grieve. I was the shadow of your face before you were born.*

I drank hot tea and shivered.

I went over and knelt down in front of the chortens erected for my sons. I suddenly doubted that I would ever understand either the natural or the spiritual dimensions of The Empty Too Much. I doubted that I would ever *belong* to either.

I knelt by the figure of the sleeping Seghers, the blinded Seghers who had, perhaps foolishly, attempted to exercise courage on my behalf. I sensed that he had lost his way, and that when he awoke it would be in a space of the Incomprehensible, a secret, inner protectorate of The Empty Too Much. I thought of how he had once told me of what he termed *The Alchemy of the Sand*; that alchemy was the process of carrying to the end something that had not yet been completed.

He slept through the night.

At the new fire of dawn his condition remained the same.

"What now?" I asked.

"You must do what you must do."

"I'm going after Gela."

"You will need a guide," he said.

Then I told him about the passing of Treml. He had not heard that news. His face blanched.

"No, *you* will need a guide," I said. "Maeleeva is in the east, and the Sisters of the Barren are headed east. It appears that fate wants to keep us together."

He smiled shyly.

"We are lived by the life forces themselves," he responded.

I nodded. Perhaps that was true.

"When your sight has been restored," I remarked, "you will need to pick up that book of yours and follow the dictation of the gods—to record that endless poem. To finish what can't be finished."

He chuckled.

"Well said," he murmured. Then, after a pause, he added, "What about Tovelmi?"

I merely shrugged.

I stood up, eager to get going, eager to take back my child from those who had stolen her. I didn't want a blood revenge. Only my beautiful daughter.

Light swept across the mouth of the cave, resplendent in gold.

I looked out at the necessary opus of the future.

And that's when I saw him.

A magnificent creature. Truly magnificent.

Cantering not more than a quarter of a mile away.

A black centaur as large as an elephant.

"Come look!" I said to Seghers.

"What do you see?"

Then, of course, I regretted my words. As graphically as possible, I described the creature that almost seemed to have been sent by the gods. When I ended my description, Seghers raised his fists in near jubilation.

"We must follow him, Mozef! We must follow him!" he cried.

And so we did.

ABOUT THE AUTHOR

Stephen Gresham has been publishing commercial fiction since 1982. His books include:

Moon Lake
Rockabye Baby
Half Moon Down
Dew Claws
The Shadow Man
Midnight Boy
Abracadabra
Runaway
Night Touch
Blood Wings
Demon's Eye
The Living Dark
Primal Instinct (Written as "John Newland")
Just Pretend (Written as "J.V. Lewton")
Called to Darkness (Written as "J.V. Lewton")
Night Shapes
Haunted Ground
In the Blood
The Fraternity
Dark Magic
The Book of Moonlight
Crossing the River of Good Mind
Deadrise
The People of the Wild
The Nahollo Chronicles:
Strangers to the Mystic Beast
The Snakehole Man
Gone to Where I Could Not Follow

Visit www.stephengresham.com

Stephen also enjoys hearing from readers at greshsl@auburn.edu.

Curious about other Crossroad Press books?
Stop by our site:
http://store.crossroadpress.com
We offer quality writing
in digital, audio, and print formats.

Enter the code FIRSTBOOK
to get 20% off your first order from our store!
Stop by today!